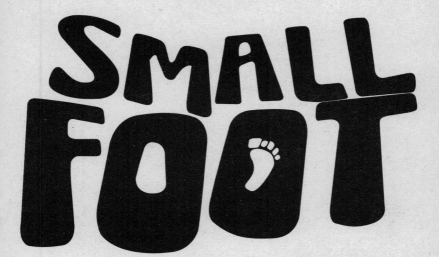

MOVIE NOVELIZATION
Adapted by Tracey West

Simon Spotlight
New York   London   Toronto   Sydney   New Delhi

SIMON SPOTLIGHT
An imprint of Simon & Schuster Children's Publishing Division
1230 Avenue of the Americas, New York, New York 10020
First Simon Spotlight paperback edition August 2018
Also available in a Simon Spotlight hardcover edition titled *Smallfoot
The Deluxe Movie Novelization*. All rights reserved, including the right of
reproduction in whole or in part in any form. SIMON SPOTLIGHT and
colophon are registered trademarks of Simon & Schuster, Inc. For information
about special discounts for bulk purchases, please contact Simon & Schuster
Special Sales at 1-866-506-1949 or business@simonandschuster.com.
Book designed by Nick Sciacca
The text of this book was set in ITC Stone Informal STD.
Manufactured in the United States of America 0718 OFF
10 9 8 7 6 5 4 3 2 1
ISBN 978-1-5344-3226-0 (pbk)
ISBN 978-1-5344-3227-7 (*Smallfoot The Deluxe Movie Novelization* hc)
ISBN 978-1-5344-3228-4 (eBook)

Prologue
Written in Stone

On the top of a very, very high mountain covered in ice and snow, a group of Yeti children sat in a circle around their village leader, the Stonekeeper. His long, white beard touched the ground. He wore a robe made of flat stones. He carried a purple crystal staff that glittered in the light of the campfire.

"The stones are here to protect us and keep us safe," the Stonekeeper said. All the Yeti children nodded. They knew the history of their world. In the beginning, the first Yetis were created when they fell out of the butt of the Sky Yak. Then they tumbled out onto an island that floated on a sea of endless clouds. And below the clouds was the Great Nothing—nothing but endless blackness. They knew they had to be vigilant to protect their island. They had to feed ice to the Mountain Mammoths who kept the island from sinking.

And every morning a gong had to be rung to wake the Great Glowing Sky Snail. The snail crawled across the sky, bringing light to the village.

All the rules of life for the Yetis were written on the stones.

The Stonekeeper looked at the children. "Who can tell me what will happen if you don't follow the stones?"

"The Smallfoot will get you!" answered Gwangi, a young Yeti with shaggy purple fur, and the Stonekeeper frowned.

"Ahhhhhhh!" the other Yeti kids shrieked with fright.

"It's a horrible creature . . . ," Gwangi continued.

"With flat white teeth," added Kolka, who wore her hair in a ponytail.

Another Yeti, smaller than the others, jumped up. "And beady little eyes!" Fleem cried.

"And the *only* hair it has is on the top of its head," Gwangi said.

"Is that really true?" asked a Yeti named Migo. He'd never heard of a Smallfoot before.

"No, Migo," said the Stonekeeper firmly. "And how do we know it's not true? Meechee, tell them."

"Yes, Father," replied a Yeti who wore her lavender hair in a long braid. She stood up. "Stone Ten tells us, 'There is no such thing as a Smallfoot.'"

"That's right," the Stonekeeper said proudly. He patted her on the head, and then removed Stone Ten from his robe.

"There is no such thing as a Smallfoot!" he said, in a voice that said the discussion was over.

Gwangi, Kolka, and Fleem grumbled, but they didn't argue with the Stonekeeper. Migo felt relieved—but still, every time he heard the stories, he had questions about things the stones didn't have answers for. Like, Why was the sky blue? And, Was there more to life than what could be found in the Yeti world?

But he knew he couldn't ask the questions, because, just like Stone Fifteen said, "Ignorance is bliss!" So he pushed them down inside him and decided to simply forget about them as best he could. And the questions stayed there for years, until Migo grew up.

Little did they realize then that in a few years, those children would become important members of their little village.

Chapter One
Doing What the Stones Say

The last grains of sand trickled from a bottle and fell onto a small wood lever that dropped on one end, raising a feather that tickled a hairy foot. The foot belonged to Migo's father, Dorgle, who was asleep in bed, until the feather tickled him. He woke up and clapped twice, and fuzzy yellow snails puffed up and glowed, lighting up the room.

He jumped out of bed and walked past his son's room.

"Migo, up and at 'em! Time to ring the gong!"

The sound of his father's voice startled the young Yeti awake. He sprang up, ready for action. Over the years he had grown to the size of a young pine tree. Shaggy white fur covered his body, from the top of his head down to the tips of his blue toes. Blue horns stuck out from the sides of his head, and when he yawned, his mouth opened to reveal enormous teeth.

"Oh yeah. Gong time!" Migo cried.

Dorgle was a head shorter than Migo, but wider and furrier, with an impressive fur mustache. As Migo followed him out of the cave, more snails lit up the darkness with their natural glow. But Migo knew it wouldn't be dark for much longer. He and his father had an important job to do.

They walked out onto a platform that looked out over the Yeti village. The other Yeti were still in their caves, waiting for the day to dawn.

Migo put a helmet on Dorgle's head, which was flat across the top, rather than pointy like his own. Then he strapped a harness to his father's chest. Dorgle climbed into a wooden seat that was part of a catapult-like contraption sitting on the platform. Migo began to turn a large paddle wheel that was attached to the seat by a rope. As Migo cranked, Dorgle's seat slowly moved backward.

"Dad, I was thinking," Migo said. "Gong Ringer is, like, a really important job, isn't it?"

"It might be *the* most important," Dorgle replied proudly.

"More than Stonekeeper?" Migo asked. "He's the leader of the whole village."

"But if I don't ring the gong, the Great Sky Snail won't rise and bring light to the village," Dorgle pointed out. "And then everyone would be in the dark, including . . ."

Migo gasped. "The Stonekeeper! And he can't do his job in the dark!"

"That's right, Son!" Dorgle said. "Let's wake 'em up." He leaned forward in the seat. "Launch!"

Migo released a lever, and the seat lurched forward, sending Dorgle flying. With perfect aim he flew through a hoop at the end of the platform and then soared over the village to his target—a huge metal gong. He hit it headfirst, and dropped to the ground.

Goooooooooooooooong!

The sound of the gong rang through the village and bounced off the mountain peaks. Dorgle got up, shaking his head, and looked hopefully at the horizon. From the platform Migo did the same.

Very slowly the rays of light began to shine in the sky.

Migo raised his arms. "Woo-hoo! Good one, Dad!" he cheered. "Look at it rise! You did it!"

Migo couldn't wait until it was his turn to bang the gong and wake the village. For now, he was happy to be helping his dad. He hopped off the platform and slid down into the village using his big Yeti feet like a pair of skis.

Snail lights were starting to come on in every cave as the Yetis woke up and got ready for a busy day. They popped their heads out of windows and doors to greet the morning light—and Migo, as he sailed past them.

Migo passed by a tall tower. At the very top, Yetis rode in a circle on unicycles, turning a wheel that made the tower spin around and around.

As the wheel spun, a pulley lifted up a block of ice—with a Yeti attached to it by his frozen tongue! The pulley dropped the Yeti—and the ice chunk—onto the top of a platform. Then the Yeti pulled his tongue off the ice block and walked away to join a group of Yetis striking an ice cliff with pickaxes.

Migo watched as a different Yeti jumped onto a chunk of ice and rode down the ice cliff, like an extreme athlete on a snowboard. She zoomed past other Yetis all doing the same thing.

When they reached the bottom of the cliff, the

ice chunks had turned into smooth balls. The snow-boarding Yetis dropped the ice balls off at a giant pile, where other Yetis polished them with their fur.

Migo smiled. "Looks like it's going to be another perfect day."

He slid down the main street of the village and skidded to a stop in front of an ice pop stand, where his dad waited for him.

"Two, please," Dorgle told Frigg, the ice pop vendor.

Frigg gave him the ice pops. Dorgle gave one to Migo, who ate his. Dorgle applied his ice pop to his aching head.

Frigg turned to Migo and asked, "Isn't today the day?"

"Yep!" Migo replied. "Just need a thumbs-up from the Stonekeeper after my practice run, and then I'm officially the assistant Gong Ringer!"

Erp, the village stonecutter, approached. "That's why you'll need this, Migo," he said, handing him a shiny new helmet.

"Thanks, Erp!" Migo said. "I'm going to go try it out. See you at home, Dad!"

"Good luck today, Migo," Frigg said.

Migo waved. "Thanks!"

He walked up the path back home, humming a happy tune. Along the way he passed some cute toddler Yetis skating on the ice, using their big feet as skates just like Migo did.

"Hey, where's Soozie?" Migo asked Spike, a young toddler Yeti with spiky hair.

"Look out below!"

Soozie barreled down a hill and hit a ramp that launched her into the air. She landed on a shop awning, bounced off, and crashed into Migo. He laughed.

"Well, the helmet works," he said, standing up and helping the young Yeti up from the ground.

He marched down the street with the little toddlers at his heels. They walked past a huge pile of the polished ice balls. On the hill above, a group of Yetis were sending the ice balls shooting down a slide made of ice.

Migo picked an ice ball up from the pile, and the toddlers did the same. Then they got in line with other Yetis holding ice balls. When it was Migo's turn, he dropped his ice ball into the mouth of a large statue.

Just then, Gwangi popped out from behind the

statue. He had grown into an enormous Yeti with a round head and body with purple shaggy fur.

"Do you ever ask yourself why we do this?" Gwangi asked. "Something's going on. I hear noises from deep within the mountain."

"The Mountain Mammoths," Soozie said. She already knew the stories of the stones.

Next, Kolka popped out from behind the statue.

"Mountain Mammoths? And you believe that?" Kolka asked.

Gwangi's eyes narrowed. "All part of the cover-up."

The kids looked at Gwangi and Kolka, wide-eyed. Migo swept them up and moved them away.

"Hey, kids, don't listen to them," Migo said. He stopped and lowered his voice. "They're a little weird."

Soozie looked back at Gwangi. "What's he saying about a cover-up?"

"Whoa, whoa. No, guys!" Migo cried. "You're questioning the stones, and you can't do that!"

Soozie frowned, and Migo understood her skepticism a little bit. But he'd learned long ago that there was no point in asking questions.

"When you have a question, just stuff it down inside," he advised. "We can make it a game! Let's try it!" He took a deep breath and motioned pushing something down.

The little Yetis copied him.

"Yay! Push! Push! Push!" the little Yetis sang out, making the same pushing motion.

"Great!" Migo said. *But maybe it isn't so great,* he thought.

The toddlers followed him as he continued his walk, deep in thought. Over the years he must have dropped thousands of ice balls into that statue's mouth. And thousands of times he'd wondered why he was doing it. And every time he'd asked, he'd gotten the same answer. . . . *Because the stones say so!*

And so he buried his questions deep inside, like he'd shown the kids how to do. It was a lot easier to just enjoy the beautiful day and the beautiful snow and not think about why things were the way they were.

"What could be better than this?" Migo asked, looking around the village. "It's perfection!"

"No it's not," said Fleem, who was still shorter than all the other Yetis his age. Migo ignored him.

Kolka appeared next to him. "There's gotta be more," she said, and Migo just kept walking.

11

Then Gwangi bounded up to them. "We should be asking *more* questions," he said, and Migo steered the toddlers away from him again.

"Ignore them," he told the kids, wanting to protect them. "Look around us. The ice is glistening. Everybody is busy and happy doing their jobs. Life really is perfect!"

His words echoed down the street, and he closed his eyes, because he knew if he said it enough, and said it loudly, it almost felt like things really were perfect.

Almost . . . , repeated a little voice inside his head, and he did what he always did. He pushed it down, and he kept going.

Chapter Two
Launch!

"Practice gong!"

Dorgle shouted the warning from the end of the launching platform. This was Migo's first time training to be the Gong Ringer, and Dorgle didn't want anybody to be confused and think that morning had started all over again. (And also he didn't want anybody to get squashed if Migo missed his target.)

Other Yetis spread the word around the village.

"Practice gong!"

"Practice gong!"

"Practice gong!"

Migo sat in the launch chair where his father had sat that morning. He strapped on his helmet.

"You ready?" Dorgle asked.

"Beyond ready!" Migo replied. "I can't wait until this is my actual job."

"You're about to join a long line of family greats. Erp, Dottard, Aunt BamBam, Grandpa Flathead," Dorgle listed, and then he got dreamy eyes. "And of course your mom. She could bang a gong like there was no tomorrow."

Migo nodded. As a tiny Yeti he'd watched his mom launch off the platform many times.

"Wish she was here to teach you," Dorgle said with a sigh.

"You're doing great, Dad," Migo assured him, and it was true. Dorgle had done a wonderful job raising Migo by himself, although the villagers had helped.

Dorgle smiled at him. "Thanks, Son."

A question popped into Migo's mind—one he knew he might not get an answer to.

"Dad, when I become Gong Ringer, will I really end up being as short as you?" he asked.

"Yep! I used to be your height," Dorgle replied.

"And will my head become flat, like yours?" he asked hopefully.

"Absolutely," Dorgle promised, and he whacked the top of his head.

Migo grinned. "Awesome!"

Dorgle leaned in to his son. "Okay, first—check your wind. It doesn't take much to blow you off course."

Migo licked his finger and held it up. He didn't feel any gusts. "Wind. Check!" he reported.

"Good. Now true your aim," Dorgle told him. "You'll mess up big-time if your aim isn't true."

Migo held a finger in front of his eye and lined it up with the giant hoop in front of the platform—the aiming circle.

"Aim. Check!"

"Great," Dorgle said. "Now, this is important. Even though you know it's gonna hurt, you gotta hit it head-on."

"Does it really hurt?" Migo asked.

Dorgle nodded. "At first, yes. But then not so much. See?" He picked up a small rock and whacked the top of his head with it. He didn't flinch.

"Cool," Migo said.

Dorgle walked back to the paddle wheel. "Say the word, Son."

Migo squinted ahead. The gong was in his sights. His heart was pounding. He was about to make his first launch!

"Launch!" Migo yelled.

Dorgle released the lever. Migo sprang forward—and then fell flat on his face.

"Did I mention you gotta keep your feet off the floor?" his dad asked.

Migo groaned. "Nope."

"Sorry," Dorgle said.

Migo got back to his feet and back into the seat. His dad cranked the wheel again. This time Migo made sure both of his feet were off the floor.

"Launch!" he cried again.

When he tried again, he flew forward—but his aim was off. He hit the edge of the hoop and fell back onto the platform.

Migo tried again.

"Launch!"

The seat flipped backward, sending Migo tumbling. He climbed into the seat and tried again.

"Launch!"

The seat didn't fly. Instead it spun around and around and around. . . .

"Launch!"

Migo launched straight up into the air, like a rocket! Dorgle gazed up after him.

"Never seen that happen," Dorgle remarked.

Migo was sore and pretty beaten up, but his spirit wasn't broken. He climbed back into the seat and gave his dad one more thumbs-up.

"Launch!"

Dorgle released the lever. Migo sailed through the air, straight through the aiming circle.

"Woo-hoo!" Migo yelled.

"Way to go, Migo!" Dorgle cheered.

What an amazing feeling! Migo thought as the air rippled through his fur. *And what an amazing view!*

The entire village spread out before him. The shops, the giant statue, the ice pile, the palace, Meechee. . . .

Meechee was standing on the palace steps with her father. It looked like she and the Stonekeeper were talking. Meechee was smiling and seated on top of her pet mammoth, Blossom. But then Meechee looked up, right at Migo. He stared back at her.

He'd had a crush on Meechee ever since they were kids. Meechee was so smart! She'd memorized all the stones before anyone else in school, and she didn't smile much, but when she did, it could melt the biggest ice chunk, Migo thought. And her hair . . . her hair was the nicest shade of lavender, and she wore it in a long, thick side braid.

She noticed me! he thought happily.

Then he heard his father's panicked voice from the platform. "Migo, true your aim! True your aim!"

Migo looked away from Meechee—and realized he was off course. But it was too late to fix the problem. He soared over the gong, and over the mountain wall that bordered the village.

Splat! He crashed into the snow.

He stood up and shook the snow off his fur. Dazed, he looked around.

He'd landed in the ice cliffs! The ice cliffs led to the edge of the world . . . and the Great Nothing.

"Uh-oh," he said, gazing around. "Not supposed to be out here."

Then he felt the cold wind on his head and realized that his helmet had flown off.

"My helmet? Where'd it go?"

He walked in a circle, trying to locate his missing helmet. Then he heard a buzzing noise coming from the clouds.

"What's that?" he wondered aloud.

Curious, he walked toward the sound until he

came to the edge of the cliff. Clouds floated in the air as far as he could see. This was where the world ended.

The buzzing noise got louder. In the distance a flash of color broke through the clouds.

Migo shielded his eyes with his hand. "Wow. What is that?" he wondered. It looked like a giant bird with wings, but no feathers.

Migo didn't know it, but he was looking at a small airplane. A trail of smoke poured from the plane's propellers. And it was heading right for Migo.

Whatever it was, it was about to crash into him!

Chapter Three
A Smallfoot!

Migo turned and ran as fast as he could. The plane zoomed toward him.

"Aaaaaah! Stop it! Get away!" Migo yelled, looking over his shoulder as the creature chased him.

Wham! The plane hit the ground behind Migo, sending up a blast of snow in its wake. Migo jumped down into a ravine to hide, but his feet hit a sheet of ice, and he slid up and launched into the air! He landed right on top of the plane and rode it like a cowboy riding a bucking bronco. Then the plane hit a bump and flung him forward, headfirst into the snow.

He popped out of the snow to see the nose of the

plane skidding toward him. It stopped inches away.

Migo sighed with relief. "Whew!"

Then the cockpit burst open and the pilot shot out of the plane. His parachute opened up, and Migo watched, wide-eyed, as the pilot slowly fell back down to the snow. The parachute covered him.

Curious, Migo slowly approached the pilot. The man crawled out from under the parachute. Migo had never seen anything like the pilot before. He was so small! And where was his fur?

"*Ahhhhhhhh!*" the pilot screamed. Startled, the man jumped back, slipped, and landed on his back with his feet facing Migo. The Yeti was amazed.

"Look at your small foot," he said, which to the pilot sounded like growls and snarls. Then it hit Migo. "Smallfoot" was a word he knew—a word from the stones. "Oh my gosh, it's a *Smallfoot*!"

Excited, Migo leaned in to take a closer look, but a blast of wind filled the parachute and sent the pilot flying away from Migo into the clouds.

"No! Come back!" Migo yelled.

The pilot was gone—but the Smallfoot's craft, the airplane, was still there.

Migo made his way to the village as fast as

he could, heading right to Main Street, yelling, "Everyone! You gotta see this! Come here!"

He stopped in the middle of the market stalls to catch his breath. Some of the Yetis noticed him, and a group of kids ran up to him.

"I. Saw. A SMALLFOOT!" Migo announced.

The Yetis all began to chatter excitedly to one another.

"What did he say?"

"He can't be serious!"

"That's impossible!"

"Just follow me and see for yourselves!" Migo said. "Come on, everybody!"

Curious, a group of Yetis followed him. Thorp, who was the Stonekeeper's son and Meechee's brother, was patrolling the village while riding on his mammoth, when he spotted them leaving. He turned toward the palace.

"Dad!" he called out.

Migo, meanwhile, couldn't wait for everyone to see the craft of the Smallfoot. But before he could get there, a hungry yak tugged on a piece of greenery near the plane. The ice cracked, and the snow underneath the plane loosened. This sent the plane tumbling down the hill, but then it stopped at the edge of the cliff, teetering.

"It came at me from the sky in some sort of hard, shiny, flying thing!" Migo was saying as he led the villagers toward the crash site. "It made a sound like—*eeeooooowwww!* It's right this way."

Migo crested a hill—just in time to see the plane fall over the cliff and disappear into the clouds.

"No, no, no!" Migo wailed. He watched helplessly as a wind blew away the tracks that the craft had made in the snow.

He turned to the other Yetis. "It was right here!" he insisted. "Look, I swear! The shiny flying thing, that's what the Smallfoot shot out of. It was like, *poof*!"

He made a parachute shape with his arms.

"And then a big fabric thing landed on top of it, and it was like, *whaaaaa!* And when it saw me, it sang the most strange, beautiful song, like, *aaaaaaaaaah!*"

"Ahh!" the Yetis repeated.

"Almost," Migo said. "It was more like, *aaaaaaaaaaah!*"

He looked around. "It's probably still around here somewhere," he said. "Let's look for it!"

One Yeti got a look of panic on his face. "Still around here?"

"It could be in the village!" someone else cried.

"It could be at my house!" someone yelled.

"GET THE CHILDREN!" another Yeti shrieked.

The Yetis started freaking out, all talking at once.

"Wait. Hold on, everyone," Migo said. "The Smallfoot didn't seem all that scary. It was kind of cute."

At that moment Thorp entered the scene, riding his mammoth. He blew on a large horn. "Everyone! Make way for my dad! I mean—the Stonekeeper!" he announced. "Sorry, Dad—uh, Stonekeeper." He shook his head. "I blew it."

The murmuring of the crowd calmed down, and the Yetis fanned out as the Stonekeeper arrived, followed by Meechee.

"Good morning, everyone. How are you?" the Stonekeeper asked.

Dorgle came running up behind them, and his stomach dropped when he saw Migo at the center of attention. This could not be good.

The nervous Yetis fired frantic worries at their leader:

"Stonekeeper! He saw a Smallfoot!"

"He said it might still be out there!"

"He said it fell from the sky."

The Stonekeeper smiled calmly. "Now, I know that Migo has gotten you all very anxious with his little 'story,'" the Stonekeeper began. "But there's nothing to fear, because it isn't true."

"But I saw one," Migo insisted.

"No you didn't," the Stonekeeper replied.

"I did," Migo pressed.

The Stonekeeper smiled. "You couldn't have seen it, because it doesn't exist."

"I know, I know. Because a stone says, 'There's no such thing as a Smallfoot,'" Migo replied.

The Stonekeeper pointed to one of the stones on his robe. "Yep. Right here. Clear as day."

"I know, but it was right there in front of me!" Migo said.

Thorp climbed down from his mammoth. "Hey, Migo. How did you know it was a Smallfoot?"

"Because . . . it had a small foot," Migo replied.

Thorp looked at his father. "Dad?"

The Yetis began to murmur. Migo sounded very sure of himself.

"Daddy, clearly he saw something," Meechee said.

"Oh, I'm not denying he saw *something*," the Stonekeeper said. He walked through the crowd, making eye contact with the villagers. "Most likely he slipped, fell on his head, got confused, and saw a yak."

The Yetis nodded in agreement.

"Because if Migo is saying he saw a Smallfoot, then he's saying that a stone is wrong," the Stonekeeper continued.

"Oh no," Migo muttered. Nobody was allowed to say that the stones were wrong.

"Is that what you're saying, Migo, that a stone is wrong?" the Stonekeeper pressed.

Before Migo could answer, his father did it for him.

"Nope!" Dorgle said loudly, pushing his way through the crowd. "He is not saying that."

He turned to the Stonekeeper. "Let me talk to him. Kids, right?"

The Stonekeeper nodded, and Dorgle pulled Migo aside.

"Migo, what are you doing?" Dorgle asked in an

urgent whisper. "Challenging the Stonekeeper? In front of the whole village?"

"Dad, what piece of advice have you always given me?" Migo asked.

Dorgle's eyebrows furrowed. "Don't eat yellow snow?"

"The other one," Migo said.

"Never pee into the wind."

Migo shook his head. "Dad, you raised me to always tell the truth."

"But if it goes against the stones, then it *can't* be true," Dorgle pointed out.

"If I say I didn't see a Smallfoot, then I'm lying," Migo said.

Dorgle looked at his son. He knew Migo believed what he was saying. Dorgle had no idea what to say.

The Stonekeeper approached them. "Migo? I thought you wanted what was best for the village," he said.

"I do!" Migo replied.

"Then are you still saying that the stone is wrong?" he asked.

The Yetis all focused on Migo, waiting for his answer.

"If saying I saw a Smallfoot means that a stone is wrong, then I . . . I guess I am," Migo said bravely.

The Stonekeeper shook his head. "Oh, Migo. It pains me to say this. It truly does. But you leave me no choice. Disobeying the stones is a grave offense. From this day forward you are banned from the village."

The Yetis gasped in shock.

"What?" Migo asked.

"Until you are ready to stand before us all and tell us the truth," the Stonekeeper said.

"I am telling the truth," Migo said.

The Stonekeeper turned to the crowd. "That's all, everyone," he said. "Back to work. Let's make it another perfect day."

Dorgle stepped in front of the village leader. "Stonekeeper! Please! That's my son."

"Just give him a little time out there to think," the leader replied. "He'll come to his senses."

Little Soozie stared up at Migo with tears in her eyes. He didn't know what to say to her. He'd been teaching the kids that the stones were always right. What would the young Yetis think of him now?

"Soozie—" he began, but Thorp rode up on his mammoth and got between them.

"Hey! You're banished!" he barked.

Migo watched all his friends walk away in disbelief.

Thorp rode away, and the other Yetis slowly made their way back to the village, leaving Migo all alone.

Chapter Four
Percy

On the same day that Migo was banished from the village, Percy Patterson was taping a segment for a television show deep in a snowy forest with his assistant, Brenda.

"Few can survive the cold, brutal environment of the Himalayas . . . but this ingenious creature defies the odds," Percy said, smiling brightly into the camera. Still smiling, he held up his left arm, where a spider was slowly making its way up to his shoulder. Dramatically he continued, "The rare Himalayan jumping spider! This week on *Percy Patterson's Wildlife*."

Brenda stood nearby and watched, nodding her head in approval as Percy kept speaking.

"This agile arachnid can lay one thousand eggs

at a time and jump fifty feet into the air!" Percy looked at his arm, shook it a bit, and then blew on the spider. It didn't move.

"Hmm. There's an element of mental preparation, I'm sure," he said.

Percy glanced up and saw that the cameraman was yawning. He glanced over at Brenda, who gave him an encouraging thumbs-up. In desperation, Percy snatched the spider off his arm and threw it on his face.

"It's attacking!" he shouted. "Oh no! The venom! It's going to my brain! I can't feel my face!" He whispered softly to Brenda and the cameraman, "Keep rolling, keep rolling." Percy clutched his throat as if he'd been poisoned.

"Cut," Brenda said.

Percy continued to ham it up for the camera. He covered one eye with his hand.

"My eye! My eye!" he yelled.

Brenda put her hand over the camera lens.

"CUT!" she shouted. "Percy, what are you doing?"

"Saving our show," Percy replied. He placed the spider back on his arm. "Me getting attacked by a spider would get fantastic ratings!"

Brenda sighed. "Percy, our show is educational and enlightening, a show that promotes respect of our fellow creatures on this planet."

"I know. That's why no one is watching it," Percy answered.

"That's why *I* don't watch it," the cameraman agreed.

"Look, Brenda, unless our spider jumps, it's boring." As if on cue, the spider jumped off Percy's arm.

"Hey! It jumped!" Percy shouted happily.

The spider landed on the cameraman, who screamed and ran straight into a wall, shattering his camera.

"Now that was exciting!" Percy said. "Did we get that on film?"

"No," the cameraman muttered.

"Of course not," Percy said. "All right. I'll just have to go over here and interview a piece of bark, shall I?"

Percy turned to leave and *WHAM!* He slammed right into the pilot, who stared up at Percy with wild eyes.

"Y-y-yeti," he said.

"What did you say?" Percy asked.

The pilot took a deep breath. "My plane . . . crashed. In the snow. Teeth, claws, huge!" He grabbed Percy by the shoulders. "I SAW A YETI!" he shouted.

Percy's face suddenly lit up. He had an idea. He smiled at the pilot.

"A Yeti, you say? Let me buy you a cup of coffee and you can tell me all about it."

The pilot looked anxiously at Percy. "You believe me, don't you?"

Percy grinned again and patted the pilot's arm reassuringly. "Of course I believe you. I can't wait for you to tell me allllll about it."

Chapter Five
We Believe You

Migo didn't know what to do. Lost in thought, he walked along the cliffs, through the ice and snow. Finally he sat down on a rock and watched the snow whirl around him. A gust of wind swirled past his ear and sounded like *Miiiigo*. Migo gasped and looked to his left, then to his right.

"Who's there?" he called out.

He heard it again.

Miiiigo.

"Smallfoot, is that you?" he said. "Ugh, maybe I am going crazy. No wonder no one believes me."

"We believe you."

Migo whipped around to see Gwangi emerge from the fog, followed by Kolka and Fleem.

"Oh, it's you guys," Migo said.

"Miiiigo," Fleem said. He turned to Gwangi and Kolka. "Is it just me, or does he look disappointed that it's us?" He leaned toward Migo. "Can't say I blame you."

"No, no. Thanks for believing me," Migo said. "But I'm starting to think that I didn't see a Smallfoot."

"You want proof that you saw what you saw?" Kolka asked.

Migo nodded. "Yeah"

"We got proof," Gwangi said.

"So you believe that I saw a Small—" Migo began, but he was interrupted by Gwangi, Kolka, and Fleem all yelling, "Sssshhhh!"

"They're listening," Gwangi said.

"Who?" Migo asked.

"The ears of oppression."

"Yeah," Kolka agreed.

"This way," Gwangi instructed. "Stealth mode."

Migo sighed. "Could this day get any more bizarre?" he asked to no one in particular. He felt something odd and looked down. Fleem was touching his fur.

"Is this too close?" Fleem asked.

"Uhhh, what?" Migo said, confused.

"You know what you are now?" Fleem asked. "One of us!" Fleem started chanting. "One of us! One of us!"

Migo sighed. He couldn't go back to the village. And Gwangi, Kolka, and Fleem might be a little strange, but they acted like they had answers for him. And right now all he had were questions.

"I guess you're all I've got, huh?" he said.

"Yeah, I know," Fleem replied. "Stinks, right?"

They caught up to Gwangi and Kolka and entered a narrow ravine.

"Where are you taking me?" Migo asked.

"Our leader requests a meeting," Kolka replied mysteriously.

"You have a leader?" Migo asked. "Who?"

Fleem's eyes gleamed. "You'll see," he said.

They reached a wall of rock. Fleem pulled a switch, and a secret entrance opened up.

"Oh boy," Migo said.

The entrance opened into a large cave. Gwangi stepped in first and clapped twice. Snails lit up the darkness, revealing a stone stairway that curved downward. They followed it down.

"He's here," Gwangi announced.

A Yeti stepped out of the shadows, and Migo gasped.

"Meechee?"

"Hi, Migo," she said. "Welcome to the secret headquarters of the S.E.S."

"It stands for 'Smallfoot Exists, Suckas!'" Fleem explained.

"Actually, it's the 'Smallfoot Evidentiary Society,'" Kolka said.

Fleem shrugged. "I mean, my name has more pizzazz."

"Smallfoot?" Migo repeated. "Wait, you're like a . . . secret society . . . about Smallfoot? But you're the Stonekeeper's daughter!"

"Look, I love my father, but he isn't exactly what you would call 'open to new ideas,'" Meechee replied.

"Because questions lead to knowledge," Kolka added.

"And knowledge is power," Gwangi said.

"Uh-huh," Migo said, his mind whirring as he tried to take everything in. He knew he wasn't supposed to ask questions. But he'd had so many of them, for as long as he could remember! And these

guys were saying that asking questions was okay.

"So, you don't just believe in the Smallfoot. . . . You've been looking for one!" he realized. That idea felt strange to him.

Meechee motioned for Migo to follow her. She led him to a map of the mountain on the wall, marked with red Xs all over it.

"See all the red Xs?" she asked. "We've been searching the entire mountain, dreaming of first contact."

"Why are you looking for Xs?" Migo asked.

Meechee rolled her eyes. "We're not looking for Xs. We're looking for Smallfoot. And you've seen one!"

The four Yetis swarmed him and bombarded him with questions.

"Tell us everything," Meechee said.

"What did it smell like?" Kolka asked.

"Did you try to communicate?" Meechee wanted to know.

"How tall was it?" Gwangi asked.

"Was it shorter than me?" Fleem asked.

"Did it only have hair on top of its head?" Kolka asked.

"Did it hypnotize you?" Gwangi asked.

"It's gotta be shorter than me, right?" Fleem repeated.

Migo backed away from them. "I don't know! It all happened so fast. I can't prove I actually saw one."

Meechee grinned. "That's where we come in. Gwangi? Show him the evidence."

Gwangi moved to a display case and whipped off the cover. Fleem put a snail on top of Gwangi's head to add some light. Gwangi took something out of the case—a tiny, puffy winter jacket.

"First item: Smallfoot pelt," Gwangi said. "We believe it sheds its skin."

Kolka removed the next item—a small, broken ski pole. She held it up to the center of her forehead so that it resembled a unicorn horn.

"Second item: a single, magical horn. Might have power in it," she said. Then her eyes got wide. "Wait a second. I'm seeing something. Walking stick? Down a hill, with wooden planks on the feet?"

She took the ski pole away from her head. "Whoa. That was crazy."

"And then there's this," Meechee said. She held up

a roll of toilet paper. "The scroll of invisible wisdom."

Kolka bowed to the scroll as Meechee unrolled it in front of Migo.

"Just imagine the amazing stuff they put on here," Meechee said.

Migo looked at the items and shook his head. "Yeah, um, sorry, but this stuff doesn't look familiar. I don't remember the horn, and the Smallfoot I saw didn't have a pelt this color. So, yep, didn't see it."

"Wait! There's one more artifact," Meechee said. "The first thing I ever found, the thing that started all of this."

She picked up a bundle of folded cloth and unwrapped it to reveal a very small boot. Migo's eyes widened. He had seen one just like it on the Smallfoot he had encountered.

"That was a trigger! He's triggered!" Kolka said.

Meechee smiled. "I knew it! You *did* see one!"

Migo couldn't deny it.

"Where did it go? Think, Migo! Think!" Meechee urged.

"Tell us!" Gwangi demanded.

"I don't know," Migo answered.

"Slap him!" Fleem cried.

"No, channel the energy!" Kolka suggested.

Migo closed his eyes, remembering. "It all happened so fast. . . ." He remembered seeing the creature's tiny foot, and then *whoosh!*

"It got whisked away in the wind," Migo explained. "Over the clouds."

"Which way?" Meechee pressed. "Up the mountain? Over to the village? To the sky? WHERE?"

In Migo's mind he could see the Smallfoot falling into the clouds.

"Down," he said.

"Did you just say 'down'?" Kolka asked.

Migo's eyes snapped open. "'Down'? No. Did I?"

Excited, Meechee hurried over to the map on the wall. She pointed to the area below the clouds.

"You did! Down! Of course!" she cried. "You know, I have always thought it was weird that a mountain floats, when there is obviously some invisible force pulling us all downward. I call it the law . . . of gravity!"

Fleem shook his head. "You really stink at naming stuff."

Meechee tapped the map. "But this explains why

we haven't found a Smallfoot up here. Because it's down there. Below the clouds." She turned to Migo. "And if we want to find that Smallfoot and change the world, that's where we need to go."

Migo's eyes widened in terror. "What?! In the Great Nothing?"

Meechee nodded slowly. Gwangi, Kolka, and Fleem nodded along with her.

"Very funny," Migo said. "You're crazy."

Gwangi's eyes narrowed. "Don't call me crazy," he growled. "Never call anyone crazy."

"Do you know why it's called 'the Great Nothing'?" Migo argued. "BECAUSE THERE'S NOTHING DOWN THERE!"

"And why do you believe that?" Meechee challenged him.

"Because it's written on the stones!" Migo replied.

"It's also written on a stone that there's no Smallfoot, and yet you saw one," Kolka pointed out.

"Yeah. Why is there a stone that says something *doesn't* exist?" Meechee asked. "Doesn't that suggest that it actually *does*? And if one stone is wrong, then others could be as well."

Migo held up his hands. "Whoa, wait. Other stones? How many do you think are wrong?"

"The whole robe," Gwangi replied.

Migo shook his head. "You know what? This whole thing's insane. I'm out."

Chapter Six
Into the Great Nothing

As he headed for the exit, Meechee ran up to him. "Migo, wait."

"Hey, I just want to prove I saw a Smallfoot so I can get un-banished," he argued. "But you want to—what? Get rid of the stones? Tear down everything our world is built on?"

"It's not just about tearing down old ideas," Meechee said. "It's about finding new ones. Don't you ever wonder what's out there?"

Migo stopped. He couldn't lie about that. He'd *always* wondered.

Meechee stared at him for a moment. "You know what? Come with me."

She stepped out of the cave, broke off two big

icicles, and handed one to Migo. Then she jumped onto the piece of ice and began to slide across the ice cliffs. Migo followed her.

"There's so much more to life than meets the eye," she told him as they zoomed along. "I think the world is so much bigger than we know."

Migo followed her down a hill, under a cliff, and into another cave. They sailed through it into a cavern, where a single tree grew. Migo blinked. How could a tree grow inside a cavern?

Meechee approached the tree and touched one of the leaves. It began to move, and Migo realized it was a dragonfly! The creature opened its wings and fluttered around the cavern.

"Sometimes things aren't what they seem to be," Meechee said with a grin.

The other "leaves" opened up and joined the other dragonfly, swirling around Migo and Meechee.

The two Yetis left the cavern and emerged back outside, where dark had fallen. Overhead a round moon shone. Meechee pointed to it.

"So, we're told that's the Eye of the Great Sky Yak, right? But what if it's not? What if it's . . . a rock?" she asked. She picked up a rock and showed it to Migo.

He frowned, confused.

"Maybe I'm wrong, but what's wrong with questioning it?" Meechee asked. "There's nothing wrong with being curious, Migo. And I know you're just as curious as I am."

Migo knew that was true. She smiled again and led him back to the edge of the cliffs, where the clouds floated in front of them.

"Life is full of wonder, Migo," she said. "Do you want to spend your life wondering if there is more to life than what we know? I don't. I want answers."

Migo gazed at the clouds. They were beautiful. And in his heart he had always wondered if there was something below them besides the Great Nothing. Before, he hadn't been brave enough to find out. But now . . .

"Down there, Migo, a world awaits," Meechee said.

Migo nodded. "Okay. I'll do it. Is there some sort of plan?"

"We're going to need some rope," Meechee replied.

Migo did a double take. "Huh?"

The next morning Migo dangled upright from a rope over the edge of the ice cliffs, while Meechee, Gwangi, Kolka, and Fleem stood watching from the ground above. The night before, the team had worked to make him a rough helmet, and they'd fashioned a harness out of some thick rope.

"Is it too late to have second thoughts?" Migo asked.

"Yes!" Fleem replied.

"I need to readjust the harness," Migo said, stalling. "It's a little too tight."

Meechee stood guard to make sure nobody was coming, while Gwangi studied the length of rope. "This should be enough."

"Should be?" Migo asked nervously.

Kolka was busy securing the end of the rope around a rock. The slack was coiled into a pile.

"We don't exactly know how far you'll need to go before you find the Smallfoot," she said. "It's also all the rope we have."

Fleem and Gwangi gripped the rope, and Meechee ran to join them.

"Okay. If we're gonna do this, we have to do this fast," she said. "Gwangi, tell him the plan."

"Listen up," Gwangi said. "Pull once to go lower, pull twice to stay put, pull three times to come up. Four pulls means you've reached the bottom and it's safe to come down."

"Wait, what was the second one?" Migo asked.

"Look, it doesn't really matter," Fleem said. He was sure the mission was going to end in disaster.

Kolka grabbed Fleem and tossed him out of the way, taking his place on the rope.

"Your safe word is 'mystical creature,'" she called down to Migo.

"That's more of a phrase, really," Migo pointed out.

"If you shout it, we'll abort the mission and pull you right up!" Kolka replied.

"How about just 'help'?" Migo suggested. "I'll scream 'HEEEELP.' Nice and short."

"You're gonna do great," Meechee told him.

Migo blushed under his furry cheeks. "Yeah? You really think so?"

"Let's do this!" Gwangi shouted.

They slowly lowered the rope. Migo's feet touched the top of the clouds.

"Migo!" Fleem called down.

"What?" Migo yelled back.

"If you die, can I have all your earthly possessions?" Fleem asked.

"FLEEM!" yelled Meechee, Kolka, and Gwangi together.

"Right. Sorry," Fleem said. "*When* you die."

They lowered Migo farther, until the clouds surrounded his whole body.

"What do you see?" Meechee asked.

"So far just seeing clouds . . . and more clouds," Migo reported. Then he gasped. "Wait! What is that?"

"Oh no!" Kolka cried.

"Sorry. Just my hand," Migo realized. "Still just clouds. And more clouds. Hey, there's a lot of clouds."

Back up on the cliff, the four Yetis heard the sound of heavy footsteps approaching. Then Thorp's voice rang out.

"Meechee, you out there?"

"Thorp!" Meechee hissed. Panicked, she let go of the rope and jumped behind a rock to hide.

"Uh-oh," Gwangi said.

Migo heard that. "Uh-oh? Why 'uh-oh'?"

Gwangi let go of the rope, and Migo dropped suddenly.

"Mystical creature!" Migo yelled.

Before they could pull Migo back up, Thorp appeared. Kolka let go of the rope now, and it slowly began to unravel.

"Hey, what are you guys doing out here?" Thorp asked.

Down below, Migo was swiftly falling. "Mystical creature!"

"What was that?" Thorp asked.

"It's, uh, the wind," Kolka replied. "It makes strange noises out here." She glanced at Gwangi and Fleem, and they all started making wind noises.

"*Oooooh . . . whiiisssshhhhh . . . mystical creatuuuuurrrrre . . .*"

Thorp stared at them, shaking his head, as the rope unraveled all the way. It went taut, catching on the rock that Kolka had anchored it to. She glanced at it, relieved that the rope had held. That meant Migo was safe. But then . . .

Snap! The rope broke.

"Ahhhhhhhhh!" the three Yetis cried.

Thorp moved forward on his mammoth.

"Stop it," he told them. "You're all acting weird. I don't like weird. Weird is . . . weird, okay?"

The mammoth's huge foot accidentally stomped on the split end of the rope before it went over the edge. The rope went taut again, slamming Migo into the side of the mountain.

"I thought I heard Migo's high-pitched kind of annoying voice before," Thorp continued. "Where is he?"

"He's dead," Fleem replied.

Gwangi stared at his friend. "Fleem?"

Fleem shrugged. "Well, he's probably dead."

Down below, Migo pulled on the rope. "How many times was up? Two? Three? Four?"

Back on the cliff Kolka slapped a hand over Fleem's mouth. "Honestly? We have no idea about the status of his whereabouts."

Thorp eyed them suspiciously. "Something's not right here," he said. "Let me think about this."

He tried to think—but gave up. "I just don't believe you. You're coming with me."

He turned to leave, and his mammoth lifted up the foot that had been anchoring the rope. The split end began to snake through the snow once more.

"Oh no!" Meechee cried, watching the scene from her hiding place.

The end of the rope fell off the cliff—and with nothing to anchor him, Migo began to plummet.

"Noooooooo!" Migo wailed. "Ahhhhhhhhhh!"

Thud! He slammed face-first into a snowbank. When he rolled over, he saw the mountain towering over him. He couldn't see his friends—just the mass of fluffy clouds separating him from them.

"Guys? GUYS?" he yelled.

He stood up and turned away from the mountain—and his jaw dropped.

"Oh wow," he breathed.

A huge, beautiful mountain range stretched across the horizon as far as he could see. Snow topped the jagged mountain peaks rising into the blue sky. Migo had never seen anything like it.

"This is so not Nothingness!" he cried. "This is definitely . . . Somethingness!"

A large bird with black wings, a red head, and a white collar of feathers soared toward him. Migo's face lit up at the beautiful sight of the condor.

"Whoa."

Naaaaaaaa!

Migo turned toward the bleating sound and saw a goat with curled horns and white, shaggy hair.

"Oh my gosh. Hi, little guy," Migo said, approaching the goat.

Naaaaaaa! the goat replied, and then Migo smiled—but then the condor swooped down and grabbed the goat in its talons.

"That is just harsh!" scolded a horrified Migo. "I'll teach you a lesson.

He quickly formed a snowball and tossed it at the bird. "Take that!" he shouted. *Pow!* It hit the condor, and the bird dropped the goat, which landed on all fours and scrambled down the mountain.

"Yes!" Migo cheered. "Run, little guy. Be free!"

Migo's eyes followed the goat—and then spotted an object in the snow.

"It's the shiny flying thing!" he said.

He quickly slid down the mountain and raced to the crashed airplane. He squeezed inside. A figure sat in one of the seats, wearing a hat.

"A Smallfoot," Migo whispered.

The figure turned around. It wasn't a Smallfoot—it was a goat!

Eeeeeeahhhhhh! the frightened animal screeched.

"Ahhhhhhhhh!" Migo screamed.

Migo jumped up—but his head hit the roof of

the plane's cockpit. The force jostled the plane, and it began to slide down the mountainside at high speed.

The plane slid into an evergreen forest and slammed into two trees, sending Migo flying out the front window. He landed in another snowbank and began to roll down a steep slope, picking up more and more snow as he rolled. He had become a giant Yeti snowball!

Wham! He hit a giant rock, launched into the air, and then landed on a rope bridge. The bridge snapped and fell under his weight. Migo grabbed the single rope that still extended across the canyon, so that he was dangling over the abyss.

Snap! The rope broke, but Migo managed to swing to the other end of the bridge. He collided with a stone pillar, which teetered, and then collapsed on top of him.

Everything went black.

Hours later Migo opened his eyes. With a groan he pushed off the broken rocks that lay on top of him, and stood up.

The moon was shining in the night sky, lighting

up the snow-covered path in front of him. And on that path Migo saw footprints—tiny footprints.

Migo paused for a moment, considering what he should do. Then he took a deep breath. He realized he had no choice. There was only one thing to do.

He followed them.

Chapter Seven
Percy's Plan

Nestled in the foothills of the Himalaya Mountains was a village of humans—containing homes, shops, and the Yak Shack, a restaurant where everyone in town liked to gather.

On the night when Migo crash-landed, Percy Patterson sat having dinner with his assistant, Brenda.

"Okay, okay, back up, back up," Brenda said. "You want to interview a man who says he saw a Yeti? And you actually believe him?"

"Of course not," Percy replied. "But it makes for good TV."

"That man probably has altitude sickness," Brenda said. "He needs help."

"After he helps us," Percy replied.

"What do you mean?" Brenda asked.

"Brenda, do you know what this village is famous for?" He pointed to a poster on the wall of a Yeti. It was surrounded by other Yeti-themed posters.

"Yetis!" he said. "More reported Yeti sightings here than anywhere else on the planet."

"So?" Brenda asked.

"Picture this," Percy said. "We're here looking for the Himalayan jumping spider, but we capture on film—a Yeti! We post the video, it goes viral, then BOOM! My ratings skyrocket!"

"Yetis don't exist," Brenda reminded him.

"Or do they?" Percy asked. He looked left and right, to make sure nobody was watching. Then he reached over to a bulging suitcase on wheels and started to unzip it. The head of a white, furry Yeti costume stared at them with plastic eyes.

"Picked up a suit in town this afternoon, and it's a cracker!" he said in a loud whisper. "It has stilts and everything!"

"You're gonna put that thing on and deceive your fans?" Brenda asked in disbelief.

"No, of course not!" he replied. "I'll be on camera,

and *you'll* put on the suit and deceive my fans."

"What? No way!"

"Brenda, please," Percy pleaded.

"Wow, what has happened to you? Where's the Percy Patterson who loved animals? Who inspired *me* to love them? Who had *integrity*!"

"I have integrity!" Percy insisted, and Brenda frowned at him.

"Okay, yes, this isn't about integrity," he admitted. "I have to do this one thing without integrity, and then I'll just be all about integrity, all the time. I will ooze integrity. I will bathe in it. I will endorse an energy drink called Integrity—not for free—but I'll donate the money to charity. That's how much integrity I'll have!"

Brenda was not going to support Percy in this. She stood up and walked away. Percy leaped in front of her.

"Brenda, no one is watching my show!" he said. "You want to save a species on the verge of extinction? Save me!"

Brenda stopped and folded her arms, waiting to be convinced.

"I used to be successful," Percy said. "*We* used

to be successful. But tracking down animals in the wild just isn't enough anymore. I can't compete with water-skiing squirrels, or monkeys riding on the backs of dogs."

Brenda nodded; he did have a point. Percy got down on his knees and closed his eyes, overcome with emotion.

"I'm desperate, Brenda," he said. "This idea is the only thing that can save us. I'm begging you to help me. I can't do this without you. Please help me!"

He opened his eyes—to see Brenda walking out the door.

"Brenda? Brenda!" Percy cried. He turned back to their table. The suitcase containing the Yeti suit was gone. "The suit! No!"

He reached for his phone and frantically dialed Brenda. If he didn't make this Yeti plan work, his career was over!

Chapter Eight
Migo Meets Percy

Migo followed the tiny footprints across the snow. Soon he heard strange music. Instinctively he kept low by rolling across the snow and hiding behind boulders so that he wouldn't be seen.

Finally he arrived at a strange wooden dwelling with a peaked roof. The music was coming from inside, and light glowed from within.

"Wow," Migo said. He crept closer to the building, and spotted the goat lurking behind the back wall, chewing on something. It looked up at Migo and kept chewing.

"Whatcha got there?" Migo asked, approaching the animal. Startled, the goat dropped what it had been chewing and bolted away. Migo picked up the

object—a sneaker. He held it up to his own foot.

"A small . . . foot," he said.

Then a creature walked out of the building. A creature with wavy brown hair and stressed-out blue eyes.

"There it is!" Migo cried. "Look at it. So majestic. So amazing. I should introduce myself. Oh, but why am I so scared?"

The Smallfoot was talking into a box, but to Migo it sounded like squeaks and chirps.

"Hmm, no language skills," Migo mused. "Didn't see that one coming."

He cautiously made his way toward the Smallfoot—Percy, who was leaving a phone message for Brenda.

"Brenda, please come back," he pleaded. "It's just this one time. I promise. Then we'll do the integrity thing. Please call me when you get this!"

Percy ended the call and glanced down to see an enormous, furry foot with blue toes. He looked up to see Migo grinning down at him.

"Thank you, Brenda!" Percy said, mistakenly thinking it was Brenda inside the Yeti suit. "You even put on the stilts! And the suit doesn't even look fake. It's quite convincing. So here's the shot. I'll film over here."

Migo heard: *Squeak, squeak! Chirp, squeak!*

"It's doing all the talking," Migo muttered. "Just say something, you idiot! Here we go."

He walked closer to Percy. "Hi. I'm Migo, and I have fallen very far—"

Percy heard: *Grrrrrr, grrooooowwl!*

"Blimey, good growl!" Percy said. "Did you put an amplifier in there or something? This is why I work with you, Brenda. When you're in, you're *all in*!"

He produced a small camera from his backpack and hit a button on it. A telescoping arm shot out, and he flipped the camera toward him so that he could film himself.

"Hair looks good, nice bit of backlight. Okay. Here we go. Yeti discovery shot, take one!" he cried.

Then his voice changed so that he sounded breathless, as though he'd been hiking for a very long time.

"Percy Patterson here, high in the Himalayas," he began. "I was looking for the rare—"

Migo's head poked into the frame as he tried to introduce himself to Percy.

"Not yet," Percy said, pushing Migo out of the way. "Okay. Cut that bit, and in three, two, one . . ."

He began the narration again. "I was looking for the rare Himalayan jumping spider, but I just heard a low growling coming from this direction."

He spun the camera around to face Migo.

"Ahhh. Is that . . . a Yeti?" Percy cried, sounding like a bad actor. Then he whispered to Migo, "Do the growl."

At that moment Percy heard the sound of an engine behind him. He whipped the camera in that direction to see Brenda, riding a snowmobile.

"Do you mind?" he asked. "Will you turn that off, Brenda? I am trying to shoot Brenda in this . . ."

His voice trailed off as the realization hit him.

"Wait a minute . . . Brenda?"

He moved the camera to Migo. Then back to Brenda. Then back to Migo.

"Hi," Migo said, but what Percy heard was, *Groooowwwwwllll!* Brenda drove off, but Percy was too terrified to notice.

"Y-y-y-y-yehht-t-t-ti." Percy could barely get the word out.

"You know, you'll laugh, because in my world everyone thinks you're a terrifying monster," Migo said. He mimed being a scary monster and growled for real this time. *Grrroooowwwwllll!*

Shaking with fear, Percy stumbled backward and fell.

"You don't look terrifying to me," Migo was saying. "You're adorable!"

Percy screamed and ran away.

"Oh, the Smallfoot song," Migo said, remembering the frightened screams of the crashed pilot. "I know this one. I know it, I know it." *Growwwllll!* "Is that not right?"

Percy ran for the door of the Yak Shack, but Migo jumped and landed in front of him. Percy turned and ran the other way, but he tripped and fell. His animal tranquilizer pistol slid out of his backpack and skidded to a stop in front of the curious goat.

"I just need to take you home and prove to everyone that you exist, so I can get un-banished," Migo tried to explain. "Okay?"

By now he had cornered Percy against the wall of the Yak Shack.

"You want to bring anything?" Migo asked.

Percy saw the goat walking away with the tranquilizer gun in his mouth. He had to get to it, somehow! He picked up a ski pole lying on the ground and hurled it at Migo.

Thunk! It stuck into the Yeti's forehead, but he didn't flinch. Percy dove through Migo's legs, slid across the snow, and grabbed the tranquilizer pistol. His hands shaking, he turned and aimed it at Migo.

"You want to bring that too?" Migo asked. "That looks cool."

Before Percy could shoot it, Migo reached out and tapped the gun. The dart fired straight up into the air! Realizing it was a good distraction, Percy broke into a run.

"Whoa, whoa, whoa, wait! Where are you going?" Migo called out. "Look how excited you are!"

Migo grabbed at Percy, but he slipped through Migo's fingers like a bar of soap. He shot up into the air, and then landed on top of Migo's head. Percy grabbed onto Migo's horns and fur, trying to find a way to bring the Yeti down.

Migo thought the little guy was playing. He flopped down onto the ground, laughing.

"Ha-ha-ha!" Migo laughed. "That tickles!"

But Percy didn't hear playful laughter. He heard only growls and grunts, and thought Migo was fighting him. He struggled desperately, trying to get away, but fate had other plans for Percy.

The tranquilizer dart sailed back down from the sky. Percy saw it coming but couldn't get out of the way.

Thump! The dart landed, piercing Percy's butt and tranquilizing him. His eyes rolled back in his head as the sleepy effect took hold. "That's ironic," he said, and then he fell over, unconscious.

"Um, Smallfoot? Hello?" Migo asked, but the Smallfoot had suddenly fallen asleep.

It wasn't a bad turn of events, actually, because now Migo could simply carry the Smallfoot back to his Yeti village. He looked at Percy's scattered belongings and picked up a sleeping bag and a length of rope. He strapped the sleeping bag to the front of his chest and then stuffed Percy inside.

"Hope you don't mind, but I'm taking you home," he told the sleeping Percy. "I'm gonna be like, 'Yo, what's up?' And they're gonna be like, 'Is that a what?' And I'm gonna be like, 'Yeah!' And their faces are gonna be like . . . 'Smallfoot exists!'"

He smiled and made his way back home.

Chapter Nine
Momma Bear

Migo happily climbed up the mountain, thinking how awesome it was going to be when everyone realized that he had been telling the truth all along.

He turned around a curve and . . . *whoosh*! A strong wind and a curtain of snow hit him. Blizzards often sprang up out of nowhere in the mountains, and now he was caught right in the middle of one.

He tried to push against the winds, but they only pushed him farther and farther back. He slid across the ice and right into a big, dry cave.

"Home would be nice, but this is good for now," Migo said. He unstrapped the sleeping bag from his chest. "Don't worry, little guy. You're safe here. Nice and war—"

Percy tumbled out of the sleeping bag and landed on the floor of the cave with a loud *clink*. Migo picked him up. Covered with ice, the Smallfoot was frozen like an ice pop!

Desperately Migo rubbed Percy against his fur to warm him up. He tapped him on the ground, trying to shatter the ice around his body.

Sticks were scattered across the floor of the cave, so he put Percy down and quickly gathered the sticks into a pile. Then he found two rocks and banged them together, creating sparks.

"Don't worry, Smallfoot. I'm going to save you. Just hang on. Hang on!" Migo urged. He banged the rocks together again, and the sparks landed on the sticks. A fire began to burn.

A few minutes later Percy's eyes fluttered open. The tranquilizer was wearing off. "Oh, fire. So warm, so nice," he mumbled.

Then he realized that his whole body was spinning. First he was facing the fire from above, and then he was lying faceup above the fire.. Then he was over the fire again. . . .

"Oh no. . . ."

Migo had created a spit over the fire and was

turning Percy on top of it like a barbecue master cooking a piece of meat. Migo just wanted Percy to warm up.

"There you go. Nice and toasty all the way around," Migo said.

"No, no, noooooooooo!" Percy screamed. He thought the Yeti was cooking him up for dinner!

"Hey, what's wrong?" Migo asked. "You hungry?"

He leaned down and grabbed an apple from Percy's backpack. Then he stuffed it into Percy's mouth.

"I'm being roasted alive!" Percy cried with his mouth full. It sounded like he was saying "I'mp pheing roaphted aliveph!" Not that it made a difference to Migo!

"Still cold? I can see why," Migo said. "You have, like, no fur." He picked up a branch and began to sweep away a layer of snow that had blown into the cave. "I'll clear off a space where you can lie until the storm passes."

He unrolled Percy's sleeping bag. "Your cocoon is almost ready," he said.

Percy struggled to free himself—and had some help from the flames, which burned through one of

the ropes binding him to the spit. He jumped off.

He'd have to make a run for it, but it wouldn't be easy getting past the huge beast. Before he tried, though, there was one thing he needed to do.

While the beast was busy, Percy turned on his phone and aimed the camera at himself, with Migo in the background.

"Percy Patterson here in what might be my last broadcast ever," he whispered. "I might get eaten. Or roasted. Or frozen solid. Or some horrible combination of the three."

He paused dramatically. "But . . . know this. I risked my life in pursuit of something extraordinary. Something bigger than us. Literally, *so* much bigger."

He focused the camera on Migo. The Yeti turned to look at him.

"Oh, great. You're moving," Migo said. "I've almost finished your—"

"I think he's saying he wants to have me for dinner," Percy guessed.

Migo turned back and continued preparing Percy's sleeping area. Percy saw his chance, and tiptoed toward the cave entrance without Migo seeing him. After blowing on his fingers to warm them up, he frantically tried to type a text.

Brenda, give me my glory, he wrote. Upload this video—and then send help!

He hit send, and the phone chimed. The words "message sending" scrolled across the screen.

Then another message appeared: "Upload time . . . 38 hours."

"Noooooooo!" Percy wailed.

A low, rumbling growl answered him. It didn't sound like the Yeti.

Percy continued to record his adventure. "Something else is here," he whispered into his phone. "Judging by the echo, I'd estimate distance is approximately two hundred meters."

He hit the flashlight app on his phone, illuminating a giant bear only six inches from his face!

"Estimations wrong!" Percy yelled, temporarily frozen in terror.

The bear roared again, loudly, her breath blowing through Percy's hair. His survival instinct kicked in, and he turned and ran—right into Migo! Terrified, Percy dropped to his knees, cowering. There was no escape!

Luckily, Migo knew what the bear was saying, even if Percy did not.

"My husband is back there sound asleep!" she growled.

"I'm sorry. I didn't know this cave was taken," Migo apologized.

"Do you know what kind of mood he's going to be in if he wakes up?" the bear asked. "I promise, it will not be pretty! Not to mention our children. It took me weeks to get them to sleep."

"I don't even have kids, but I can imagine that is just a really hard thing to do," Migo replied.

They're fighting over who gets to eat me! Percy thought.

Then Migo's big foot moved and hovered over Percy.

He's going to crush me!

Instead Migo motioned for Percy to look behind him. The bright moon shone outside. The storm had passed.

Seeing his chance, Percy made a run for it while Migo kept the bear busy talking.

"Well, gotta go," Migo said finally. "Again, very, very sorry."

Percy made it to the cave entrance, with Migo running at his heels. Percy had gotten a few feet outside the cave when he heard a loud snap behind him, followed by a pitiful roar.

Percy turned. The Yeti was caught in a bear trap! The creature was sitting on the ground, howling in pain. Percy paused.

"Don't be stupid, Percy," he scolded himself. "Do not go back to help the ferocious Yeti. Don't do it!"

"*Owwwwwwwww!*" Migo wailed.

"Although, he did just save you from a bear," Percy said. He sighed. "This is the wrong time to grow a conscience."

He hurried back to Migo, who held up his foot. The big bear trap had caught on his big toe. The Yeti tried to remove the trap, but it made him cry out in pain.

Percy's heart melted, and he patted the Yeti gently. "It's okay, big fella. Let's get this thing off."

Migo smiled gratefully. He understood that the Smallfoot wanted to help him.

"Does this hurt?" Percy asked. He pried open the trap.

"Ouch!" Migo cried. Then he looked down at his toe, where a teeny drop of blood was forming. His eyes rolled back in his head, and he passed out.

When his eyes opened again, he saw Percy wrapping his toe in a bandage. He smiled at the Smallfoot, and Percy smiled back.

"The storm has lifted," Migo said. "What do you say we get up that mountain and prove you exist, huh?"

Percy stared at Migo blankly, and finally Migo realized something.

"You don't understand a word I'm saying, do you?" he asked.

Percy's blank stare didn't change. Migo sighed and strapped the sleeping bag back to his chest and pointed at it. Percy flipped on his phone. "Okay, this is unbelievable, but I think the Yeti is actually trying to communicate with me. I think he wants me to go with him."

Migo growled and pointed to the sleeping bag again. Percy, an adventurer at heart, jumped inside.

"This is either the bravest thing I've ever done, or the stupidest," he reasoned. "Here's hoping it's the former."

"Oh, I almost forgot," Migo said.

Migo had grabbed some smoldering rocks from the fire. He dropped them into the sleeping bag.

"These should keep you warm," Migo said.

Percy flinched at the idea of the hot rocks, but he quickly realized that they were warm and toasty.

"That's actually quite nice," he remarked.

Then Migo began to bound up the mountainside.

"Almost there," Migo promised. "Meechee is gonna be so happy!"

Chapter Ten
Reunion

The members of the S.E.S. had not given up on their friend. Meechee was dangling over the ice cliffs on the rope, anchored by Gwangi, Kolka, and Fleem.

"Drop me!" Meechee cried. Then she mumbled to herself, "Quick, before I change my mind."

She looked down. "This is terrifying. I can't believe Migo did this."

"Which is why maybe, you know, you shouldn't," Kolka said. "This doesn't feel right, Meech!"

"Look, Migo is down there," Meechee said. "He might be lost or hurt."

"Or dead," Fleem added.

"Fleem!" the other Yetis scolded.

"Oh, what? Now we're not about finding the

truth?" Fleem asked. "I'm just being honest."

"I still say I should go," Gwangi said. "I'm strong-est and most prepared. I've trained myself to sleep with my eyes open. I'm asleep right now."

"We've been through this," Meechee reminded him. "He's down there because I convinced him to go, so just lower me down so I can look around. Last time we dropped him because Thorp showed up, which he might do again, so let's go!"

While Meechee talked, Migo was making his way up the mountain. He was so close that he could hear Meechee's voice.

"Guys?" he called out.

Meechee didn't hear him. "I won't be able to live with myself if I don't at least try," she continued.

"GUYS!" Migo shouted.

"Ooh, I can still hear his voice in my head," Kolka said.

"GUYS!" Migo repeated.

"It's in my head too," Gwangi said.

Meechee looked down and saw Migo climbing up toward them. "Migo! He's here!" she shouted.

Kolka put her furry hand over her heart. "I know. And he always will be."

"No, he's here!" Meechee said, pointing. "As in *over there*!"

Gwangi looked down and saw Migo. Startled, he let go of the rope, and Meechee began to drop.

"Ahhhhh! Mystical creature!" Meechee yelled.

Gwangi quickly grabbed hold of the rope again. "I've got you!"

He pulled the rope with such force that Meechee swung up in the air and landed back on the cliff—right at the moment when Migo climbed up. She ran to him and gave him a big hug.

"Migo! I'm so relieved!"

Gwangi, Kolka, and Fleem joined them and flung their arms around both Yetis.

"Migo, my brother!" Gwangi said.

"Ooh, you're alive!" Kolka squealed. "My visions had you dead, but I'm so happy they were wrong."

"See, I told you he was alive," Fleem fibbed. "Migo! I may or may not have taken some of your stuff."

While Migo was happy to see them, he gently pushed them away. "Whoa, guys. Easy."

His friends slowly backed up, and that was when they noticed the sleeping bag strapped to Migo's chest. Percy's nose stuck out of the top.

Meechee's eyes got wide. "Is that . . ."

Migo unstrapped the sleeping bag. "Smallfoot Evidentiary Society, meet your mystical creature!" he announced.

He triumphantly set the sleeping bag on top of a rock. Percy wriggled around inside the bag, unable to get out.

"Uh, I hate to tell you this, but the Smallfoot doesn't even have feet," Gwangi said.

Then Percy managed to slide out of the sleeping bag as the circle of Yetis surrounded him. Quickly he got to his feet and began to film with his camera.

"Whoa! Four more Yetis," he narrated. "It's a whole squad! Oh, this is big. This is huge!"

He moved in a circle, getting them all on film.

"I knew it was real," Meechee said, staring at Percy.

"I'm not crazy," Gwangi said happily.

Kolka fought back tears. "It is so . . . beautiful."

"And so short!" Fleem added. "I mean, it's a lot shorter than me. I love it." He approached Percy and raised his arms. "Fear me, creature! I am your god!"

"Fleem, what are you doing?" Kolka asked.

"Establishing dominance," Fleem replied.

"No, we don't dominate. We welcome it with open arms," she said. She opened her arms wide—and accidentally knocked Percy off the rock! "Are you kidding? Did I just do that?"

She picked him up and pulled him into a hug. Percy's face turned red as she squeezed the air out of him.

"Can I hold it?" Gwangi asked.

Kolka handed him over. "Sure. Here. Support the head," she instructed. "There you go."

Gwangi rocked Percy in his arms, and he and Kolka oohed and aahed over him like a newborn baby.

Meechee looked at Migo. "I can't believe you did this," she said. "You did it, Migo. You really did it."

"I'd kinda like to think *we* did it," he replied.

"We?" Meechee asked.

"Well, someone had to drop me off a cliff," Migo answered.

Meechee nodded. "So, what was it like down there?"

"Meechee, there are answers to questions even you haven't asked," he replied.

She looked at him in awe. Gwangi turned to face them.

"We gotta bring this truth to the village!" he said. "Blow some tiny minds!"

Migo looked up the at the bright moon sinking into the horizon.

"Gwangi's right," Migo said. "Let's wake 'em up!"

Chapter Eleven
Behold the Smallfoot!

In the village the feather alarm tickled Dorgle's foot. He woke up and sat up in bed.

"Up and at 'em, Migo! Time to ring the gong!" he called out.

He walked past Migo's room, made his way to the launchpad, and strapped on his helmet. Then, with all his might, he pushed the chair into launch position and climbed in.

"Aaaaand launch," he said, but nothing happened. Without Migo to pull the lever, the chair wouldn't take off.

"Migo?"

He looked behind him, and then he realized. "Oh yeah. Banished."

He knew he'd have to hit the lever himself. He reached behind, twisting and turning, but he couldn't reach it. He stretched out his leg and hit the lever with his big toe.

Sproing! The seat flung forward, firing him at the gong. But Dorgle's aim was way off. He bent his body and flapped his arms, trying to correct his course.

It didn't work. *Splat!* He crashed into the side of the gong tower, splitting his helmet in two. Then he slid to the ground.

Dorgle started to panic. No gong meant the Great Sky Snail wouldn't wake up! They would spend the day in darkness! He'd have to get up and try again.

But when he got to his feet, the first golden rays of the Great Sky Snail were shedding light on the dark sky.

He stared, dumbfounded. "What the . . ."

All over the village, snails began to glow and Yetis started to wake up.

"What just happened?" Dorgle wondered. He hadn't rung the gong, and yet the Great Sky Snail was awake.

He turned toward the village gate and squinted as a group of Yetis strolled through. One of them looked very familiar.

"Migo?" he asked.

Migo, Meechee, Gwangi, Kolka, and Fleem strolled through the village as curious Yetis stepped out of their homes. The five friends strutted down the icy street with confidence, like they were the coolest Yetis on the planet. They'd just found a Smallfoot!

Migo turned and spoke to everyone he saw. "Hey, listen, everyone. Stop what you're doing and follow us. This is going to be the best part of your day!"

Meanwhile, as soon as the sun had risen without the gong, the Stonekeeper had sent Thorp out to investigate. The big Yeti stomped down the street—and spotted Migo.

"Hey, Migo, welcome back!" he said, and then he remembered. "Wait, aren't you supposed to be banished?"

"Yep!" Migo replied cheerfully.

"Oh cool," Thorp said. "Wait, what?"

Migo and the others marched to the tree in the center of the village. By now they'd gotten the attention of the entire village. The Yetis gathered round, sensing that something exciting was about to happen.

"Everyone, come here! Gather round. I promise you are gonna want to see this!" Migo declared.

By now the entire village had gathered around him.

"Fellow Yetis!" Migo began. "There are moments in our lives that are so important that we must pause and look deeper into the moment of the pace in which we are . . . to hold such beauteous gravitas, and take in the beauty—"

"Get to the point!" someone yelled.

"Yep. Okay. Here we go. Fellow Yetis! Behold the Smallfoot!"

Migo lifted Percy up over his head and removed his boot.

The Yetis gasped. Then they all began to talk at once.

"Is that . . ."

"Can it be?"

"Whoa!"

"It has a freakishly small foot!"

The toddlers climbed on top of one another, hoping to get a better look.

Percy didn't mind being on display. He filmed the Yetis all gaping at him in awe.

"I can't believe my eyes," he murmured. "These aren't primitive beasts living in caves. This is a complex civilization! Do you know what that means for the world?"

He looked into the camera lens. "A Percy Patterson network special! You're welcome, world!"

Then the Stonekeeper made his way through the crowd. The Yetis respectfully moved aside and quieted down.

"So what's all of this excitement?" the Stonekeeper asked.

"Migo found a Smallfoot!" one of the Yetis replied.

"That's one guess," the Stonekeeper said calmly.

Migo's jaw dropped. How could the Stonekeeper deny what was right in front of his eyes?

"But, Dad, look at its small foot!" Meechee said, pointing to Percy's foot.

The Stonekeeper shrugged. "Don't yaks have small feet?" he asked. He reached out toward Percy. "Let me take it into the palace, consult the stones, and determine what it is."

Migo and the others glared at him.

"What if it *is* a Smallfoot?" a Yeti named Garry blurted out. "Does that mean a stone is wrong?"

Gwangi fake-coughed into his hand. "They're all wrong."

The villagers began to murmur to one another. Garry had a good point.

"Everyone, please!" the Stonekeeper cried. "What do the stones tell us about questions? That we take them in . . ." He took a deep breath, and then made a pushing motion with his hands. "And push them down."

The Yetis all took a deep breath—but they *didn't* push down their questions. Instead they ran to Migo, and their questions poured out like water from a faucet.

"Migo, is it dangerous?"

"Can I pet it?"

"Does it do tricks?"

"WHAT IS HAPPENING?"

"What other stones are wrong?"

Garry grabbed his head in pain. "I have so many questions!"

The Stonekeeper had lost control. Migo sat down on a rock underneath the tree and talked to the Yetis, while Percy happily filmed it all.

"Where is it from?"

"Why is it pink?"

"How did you get it here?"

"What does it eat?"

"How does it think with such a tiny little brain?"

"Honestly?" Migo replied. "I have just as many questions as you do."

A rock fruit peddler offered a rock fruit to Migo.

"Is it hungry? Does it want a bite of fruit?"

A female Yeti looked at Percy in wonder. "How is it here if a stone says it can't be?"

Migo hoisted Percy onto his shoulder and carried him through the village streets, flanked by Meechee, Gwangi, Kolka, and Fleem. A fever of curiosity was spreading among the Yetis. They had spent their lives pushing down questions, and now the questions were all spilling out. Suddenly they had questions about everything and wanted to ask them! Migo beamed. He loved seeing how excited all the Yetis were. It felt great.

The Yetis on unicycles stopped pedaling. The ice-chopping Yetis stopped chopping. The ice ball polishing Yetis stopped polishing. They looked at the world around them with new eyes.

"Is that really a snail?" one Yeti asked, looking at the sun.

"What if it's not?" another Yeti wondered.

Migo put Percy's backpack down for a moment. A few toddler Yetis raced forward and rummaged through it, inspecting each item. Percy was trying to explain what they were.

"That's a snood! It's sort of like a scarf. And that's a sock. It's sort of like a lining between your foot and your shoe."

One of the toddlers stared at Percy as he slurped up the sock like a strand of spaghetti.

"Okay, that's really not what you're supposed to . . . okay," Percy said.

Gwangi was suddenly standing in front of Percy. He handed him the roll of toilet paper. "The scroll of invisible wisdom," he announced to the Yetis.

"Oh! That will do quite nicely," Percy said. He took the roll and ran behind a rock.

"It doesn't yet trust us with its wisdom," Gwangi said.

Fleem followed Percy behind the rock to see what he was doing. He quickly returned to the Yetis with a disgusted look on his face.

"It is not wisdom, and it is definitely not invisible," he said.

Dorgle joined the crowd, nervously listening and

watching. His son was really stirring things up!

The procession continued to the palace. One Yeti stepped in front of Migo.

"If the stone is wrong, could another be as well?" she asked.

Dorgle gulped. He turned to see the Stonekeeper towering over him, glowering. Did the Stonekeeper know that Dorgle had missed the gong? Anxious, Dorgle scurried away.

The Stonekeeper looked down at his daughter. "Do you see what you've started?"

"Yes!" Meechee replied with a confident smile. "Do you?"

The Stonekeeper shook his head. "You have no idea what you've done to them."

"They're just curious," Meechee countered. "What's wrong with that?"

The Stonekeeper's gaze traveled around the village. The Yeti had not only stopped working, but were also trying new things. One Yeti hollowed out a ball of ice to make a drum. Another had carved a xylophone out of ice. The drummer started drumming, and the other played a happy melody on the xylophone. The Stonekeeper heaved a heavy sigh.

"Daddy, they have questions," Meechee said. "And you can give them answers. Be a great leader and give them what they need."

He nodded. "You're right, sweetie. That's what I intend to do."

Meechee hugged him. "Thank you."

She thought her father was on her side, but the Stonekeeper had other thoughts. The turret had stopped turning. The ice elevators weren't moving. And nobody was dropping ice balls into the statue's mouth.

He knew what he had to do.

He had to get the villagers to stop asking questions, before there would be consequences.

Chapter Twelve
The Cave of Secrets

Migo left Percy with Meechee and went to find his dad. In the excitement, he'd forgotten that his father must have been worried about him. He found Dorgle sitting on the rim of the aiming circle. Migo climbed out onto the platform and joined him.

"Migo, what do I do?" Dorgle asked, gazing at the pieces of broken helmet in his hands. "I missed the gong. But the Sky Snail came up anyway."

Migo didn't take this as bad news. "So another stone is wrong?" he asked. "This is amazing."

"What's so amazing about it?" Dorgle asked. "The stones are supposed to be . . . stones! You know? Reliable. Sturdy. Like your mother's ankles were. And now the snail is rising on its own?"

"If it's even a snail," Migo said. "Meechee thinks it might be a flaming ball of gas."

"GAS?" Dorgle wailed. "I've been banging my head on that thing to wake up a gas ball? That's usually what wakes *me* up."

"Dad, I know all this change is scary," Migo said. "But being with everyone today, asking questions, thinking, wondering—I've never felt so alive!"

"But if I don't ring the gong, I'm not the Gong Ringer," Dorgle said. "And if I'm not the Gong Ringer, then what am I?"

Migo didn't have an answer for that. The father and son sat in silence for a moment, thinking. Then Thorp called up to them from below.

"Migo! My dad wants to see you, pronto!" he barked.

Migo hurried to the palace, where the Stonekeeper waited for him on the steps. Gwangi, Kolka, and Fleem observed them from nearby.

"What's up with that?" Gwangi wondered.

"No, what's up with *that*?" Kolka asked.

She pointed toward the turrets, where Thorp pedaled a unicycle, slowly moving them all by himself.

Gwangi and Kolka exchanged glances. They both

knew that moving the tower must be really important if Thorp was trying to get it going.

"What? What am I missing?" Fleem asked.

Without answering him, Gwangi and Kolka turned toward the palace entrance.

The Stonekeeper led Migo inside and walked him through the great hall, past a line of statues.

"Look at them. The great Stonekeepers of the past," the Stonekeeper said. "Each one adding new stones as they received wisdom about what was best for the village."

Migo studied the statues. The earliest Stonekeeper wore a single stone as a necklace. The next one wore a vest of stones. With each Stonekeeper, more and more stones had been added as more rules had been made.

"The robe looks heavy," Migo said, nodding to the Stonekeeper's robe of stones, which touched the floor.

"Oh, it is," he replied. "It requires a strong backbone."

He stopped at the end of the great hall and stuck the bottom of his purple staff into a hole in the floor. Then he turned the staff. Behind them a wall lowered from the ceiling, creating a small room with no visible exit.

Then the Stonekeeper twisted the staff in the other direction. The sound of rock grinding on rock groaned as the floor beneath their feet sank, revealing a stone spiral staircase.

Migo's eyes widened. "Whoa, secret stairs."

The Stonekeeper motioned for Migo to go ahead.

"Where are you taking me?" Migo asked as they walked down the dark staircase.

"You have so many questions," the Stonekeeper replied. "I think it's about time I gave you some answers."

The stairway ended, and the landing opened into a massive cavern that housed a collection of Smallfoot objects: airplane parts, a scrap of a hot-air balloon basket, a metal piece of a satellite. Migo didn't know what they were, but it was clear that they were not from the Yeti world.

"These are Smallfoot things," Migo said. "But where did they come from?"

"Our ancestors brought them," the Stonekeeper said.

He banged his staff on the ground twice, and

snails lit up, revealing a wall carved with images. The pictures looked like they told a story.

"You see, Migo, there was a time when Yetis lived beneath the clouds," the Stonekeeper explained. "We lived happily for a long time, until we came across a group of Smallfoot—also known as humans."

Migo studied the wall to see carvings of humans with spears chasing Yetis.

"They attacked with their spears, and their sticks of smoke and thunder," the Stonekeeper continued. "They called us Sasquatch. They called us Abominable. They chased us and tried to hurt us."

Migo couldn't believe what he was seeing. His Smallfoot wasn't dangerous. He had helped Migo when he was hurt! Could these humans really have tried to hurt Yetis?

"We had to run and hide," the Stonekeeper said. "So we climbed this mountain, where we knew the Smallfoot could not survive. And then the first stone was written: 'Our world is an island that floats on a sea of endless clouds.'"

The wall carvings showed the Yeti mountain, surrounded by a ring of clouds.

"Then we wrote more laws," the Stonekeeper

explained. "It was the only way to protect ourselves from the humans. So it's just best to leave things the way they are."

"But my Smallfoot—he's not like that," Migo protested.

"They're *all* like that," the Stonekeeper replied. "Tell me, when you found him, did he meet you with open arms?"

Migo thought back to his first encounter with the Smallfoot. He had thrown a ski pole at Migo—or had it been a spear? And he'd tried to fire a gun at Migo, just like the gun in the carving on the wall. (It had been a tranquilizer gun, but Migo didn't know that.)

"They don't care about us," the Stonekeeper said, "which is why we must protect our future."

He slammed his staff into another slot on the floor and pushed down. The wall opened up, and a hiss of hot air hit Migo's face. The sound of rhythmic clinking called to him from inside a room full of steam.

The Stonekeeper motioned for Migo to enter, and he obeyed. After a few feet the steam cleared, and Migo stared at a big, strange machine.

Part of the machine was a giant fan, its blades

slowly turning. The machine sat in a huge hole bored out of the mountain, and continued to pump out steam. Through the fan the two Yeti could see a blanket of clouds stretched across the blue sky.

"Wait, are we below the clouds?" Migo asked, confused. "Our village is above the clouds."

"Or so it would seem, but look closer," the Stonekeeper said.

The truth suddenly hit Migo. "Those aren't clouds. It's steam!"

The Stonekeeper smiled. "The stones are working," he said.

"The stones?" Migo asked.

The Stonekeeper led him around the corner, to where another machine hummed.

"You might think that the jobs in this village are pointless," the Stonekeeper went on. "But each one is important. Every task insures that this machine keeps churning to make the clouds. Those below the clouds won't look up—and those above the clouds won't look down."

Migo looked at the second big machine. Ice balls dropped from the machine into an enormous cauldron, where they melted and became water. A beam of light shone on the cauldron, creating steam. The fan turned the steam into the clouds that surrounded and hid the mountain.

Migo looked at the whirring blades of the fan, which were connected to long rods that stretched way, way up. That was when it hit him—the Yetis riding unicycles had been turning the turret that powered the fan!

"So none of these stones are true?" Migo asked. "They're all lies?"

"Good lies," the Stonekeeper replied. "To protect our world."

Migo thought of all the Yetis, and how excited and happy they'd been to see the Smallfoot. How they had come alive when they'd started asking questions.

"They need to know the truth," Migo said.

"Oh, do they?" the Stonekeeper asked. "I was young once too, Migo. But as I got older, I realized that the need to protect the Yetis was more important than any misguided search for the truth."

Migo shook his head. "But the truth is important."

"Protect the lie, and you protect our village," the Stonekeeper said. "Lives are at stake, Migo. Your

friends, your father, Meechee. You want to protect them, don't you?"

Migo felt a heavy weight on his heart. The truth was important. But so was being safe.

He sighed. "So, what do you want me to do?"

"Tell everyone you were lying about the Smallfoot," the Stonekeeper replied.

"But they've already seen it," Migo argued. "They're not going to believe me."

The Stonekeeper grinned. "You'd be surprised what they'll believe."

Migo turned to the carvings on the cave wall and stared at the drawings of the humans hunting the Yeti.

"Knowledge is power, Migo," the Stonekeeper said. "The question is, What are you going to do with all that power?"

Migo didn't know. He was sure of only one thing: this was the hardest decision he'd ever had to make in his life!

Chapter Thirteen
Betrayal

Gwangi, Kolka, and Fleem had known something was up when they'd seen Thorp trying to keep the turrets spinning all by himself—and when the Stonekeeper had brought Migo inside the palace.

It had been Fleem's idea to slide down the ice ball tunnel and see where it led, so he went first. He landed inside the hidden room of the palace, in front of the giant fan. Gwangi and Kolka landed on top of him.

The three friends stared at the machine for a moment, stunned. Then Gwangi turned to Kolka. "And everyone thought I was crazy."

Meanwhile, Meechee had taken Percy back to her home. Now in her room, the Stonekeeper's daughter was trying to learn all she could from the Smallfoot. Because they didn't speak the same language, Percy drew a series of pictures for her, in order to describe the human world. Meechee tacked the drawings all over her wall and studied them while Percy filmed her.

"Okay, it's a little fuzzy, but I think I'm starting to put it together," she said. "You live in a 'city' which is part of a 'country' which is one of several countries that make up an entire world."

Although all Percy heard were growls, he had an idea that this Yeti was very smart. Fascinated, he tried to keep the camera focused on her, but his hands were shaking and his whole body was shivering.

"C'mon, P-P-Percy. Steady, mate," he told himself. "Crikey, it's cold up here!"

He lowered the camera to fix the focus, but Meechee looked blurry to him without the camera too.

"And your job is to tell stories to the Smallfoot through a small box that transmits pictures through the air in some sort of binary code system that projects a series of colored images in rapid succession at a constant rate, which is your main form of

entertainment," Meechee rattled on. She turned to Percy. "Am I even close?"

Percy wobbled toward the wall of drawings. "You're an amazing creature. I wish I could stay, but the cold, the altitude—I'm not well. Feeling poorly, understand?"

He pointed to a drawing of a house with a roof. "Home. Hoooooommme."

He motioned to Meechee's room, then made a triangle shape with his hands, and then pointed down.

"Down the mountain," Percy said. "Down."

Meechee gazed at the house drawing and nodded. "I get it," she said. "Home. And you need to get there to feel better."

Migo heard Meechee's voice as he walked through the palace halls. He entered her room and found her with Percy, who was shivering under a blanket.

"Migo! Look!" Meechee pointed to the drawings. "I figured out how to communicate with it! I've learned so much about it and its culture. This is a Smallfoot cave. I think they call it a 'house,' but I could be way off. And these are more Smallfoot."

She pointed to some stick-figure drawings of humans that Percy had made, to give her some

idea of how many humans were actually out there. Meechee was smiling, excited, but Migo imagined them all carrying spears.

"But look. I don't think this Smallfoot is well," Meechee told him. "He's cold, and his breathing is off."

Migo heard the Stonekeeper's voice in his head.

We knew that up here, the Smallfoot could not survive.

"We need to take him home," Meechee said.

"What? No!" Migo protested.

He swept Percy up in his arms. The Smallfoot could not go back to his world! If he did, the Yetis' whole village would be in danger!

"Why not?" Meechee asked. "There might be more down there. I want to see it! What was it like? Did you see homes like this? Is this what their caves look like?"

Migo couldn't tell her the truth. "Just . . . stop asking questions!" he snapped.

Meechee flinched, hurt by his words. "Stop asking questions?"

Behind them, Fleem's head bounced into view at Meechee's window. Then he dropped out of sight. Migo and Meechee hadn't seen him disappear.

"Yes! There are things you don't understand," Migo said.

"Try me," Meechee shot back.

Fleem bounced into view again. "Meechee!"

This time they noticed him. Meechee ran to the window and saw Fleem drop into Gwangi's arms. The big Yeti prepared to hurl Fleem up again, but stopped when he saw Meechee.

"Meechee, you won't believe what we found!" Kolka called up to her in a loud whisper.

"There's a machine right beneath us, and it makes the clouds!" Gwangi finished.

"Oh sure, *you* tell her," Kolka said, and sulked.

Meechee turned to Migo, who looked panicked.

"Migo, did you know about this?" Meechee asked.

"I told you to stop asking questions!" he said, and then he ran off with Percy. Percy looked up at Migo as though he wanted to say something, then passed out.

Gwangi's loud whisper had reached several other Yeti ears, and now rumors of the cloud machine were swirling around the village. A Yeti named Peaches approached Gwangi, Kolka, and Fleem.

"What did you say this machine was?" she asked.

Gwangi looked uneasy.

"Well, I guess this is happening," Fleem said.

Gwangi took a deep breath and bravely stepped forward. "Okay, listen up," he began. "Everything you thought, you better rethink your thinking, 'cause I'm about to blow your minds."

A small crowd had gathered around him.

"We. Make. The. Clouds!" Gwangi announced.

Migo ran up, carrying Percy under one arm, and burst into laughter.

"Good one, guys," he said. "Quit pranking us. We're not *that* gullible."

"What's 'gullible'?" Gwangi asked.

Kolka put her hands on her hips. "Migo, what are you doing?"

"Trust me, okay?" he said, leaning in to whisper to them. "You need to stop."

"But this is big," Kolka reminded him.

Gwangi waved to the crowd. "Come on! We'll show you!"

Migo quickly stepped between Gwangi and the crowd. "No, stop!" he yelled. "Oh sure, yeah! Let's follow crazy Gwangi to the magical cave with the

underground cloud machine that's right next to a poison ice maker that's corrupting our minds."

"Wait, what?" Fleem asked.

"None of what these guys are saying is true!" Migo shouted.

Meechee stared at him. "Migo? Why are you saying that?"

"Yeah, you haven't even seen it!" Gwangi growled angrily. "Or maybe you have."

"No, I haven't," Migo replied.

"Well, then how do you know it's not true?" Kolka asked.

"Because it's in the stones!" Migo cried.

He hated to do it. He hated the betrayed looks on his friends' faces. But at that moment he felt the Stonekeeper was right. The secret had to be kept.

The crowd quieted down when Migo mentioned the stones.

"And if we don't follow the stones, really, really bad things can happen," Migo finished.

"Well said, Migo!" The Stonekeeper stepped out of the palace. "You see, everyone? Migo has realized the strength and security that the stones give us, which is why he is officially un-banished."

Migo looked at Meechee. "Isn't that great? I think we should just focus on that more. The good news."

She turned away from him and spoke to her father. "What about the Smallfoot? You can't deny he's real. I mean, he's right here! We can all see it!"

"Tell her, Migo," the Stonekeeper said.

Migo looked down at his feet. "Uh, it's not a Smallfoot," he said. "I was wrong. It's a yak."

The Yetis began to murmur. Meechee stepped back away from Migo, hurt.

Migo held Percy up over his head. "The Stonekeeper was right," he announced. "I slipped and fell and got something in my eye, and this is what I saw on the cliffs. A pygmy hairless yak."

Percy, meanwhile, woke up for a moment.

"Feeling a bit woozy . . . ," he said weakly.

The Yetis looked confused and disappointed.

"You know that's not true, Migo," Gwangi said.

"It is true," Migo retorted with as much conviction as he could muster. He appealed to the crowd, pointing to his friends. "These guys will tell you it's not true. But you know them. They're the village weirdos. They're just . . . straight-up crazy."

The words crushed Gwangi, Kolka, and Fleem. But Meechee's eyes narrowed in suspicion.

"Why are you lying?" she asked him.

Migo knew that the villagers might think Gwangi, Kolka, and Fleem were weird, but they loved and respected Meechee. He had to make sure they didn't believe her—for their own good. For Meechee's own good. The mental image of the humans and their weapons spurred him on.

"Oh, I'm the liar?" Migo countered. "Who's been lying to her dad the whole time?"

Meechee shot daggers from her eyes at Migo.

"Meechee, lying about what?" the Stonekeeper asked.

Meechee took a deep breath and went to stand with her friends.

"We have a secret society," she told him. "S.E.S. The Smallfoot Evidentiary Society, dedicated to finding the truth about the Smallfoot. And I'm the leader."

Her father's face fell.

"I'm one of them, and I'm proud to be," Meechee continued. "I had no choice. You wouldn't listen to me. So, what are you going to do? You going to banish your own daughter?"

"Yes," the Stonekeeper said flatly.

The Yetis gasped.

"To your room," he said.

Thorp moved toward his sister, but Meechee brushed him off. "I know where my room is, Thorp."

She headed inside the palace, and the Stonekeeper faced Gwangi, Kolka, and Fleem.

"And you three. Recant your false claims and tell the truth, or suffer the consequences," he said.

"The truth?" Gwangi repeated. "I don't think anyone around here really cares what that is."

Thorp then escorted the three Yetis out of the village, and the remaining villagers turned their eyes to the Stonekeeper.

"Everyone, back to work!" he commanded, but then his voice softened. "Let's make it another perfect day."

Confused and unsure, the crowd nodded obediently at their leader and slowly began to return to their jobs.

"Now we can go back to the way things were, before this ever happened," the Stonekeeper said. He nodded to Thorp, who took Percy from Migo and walked into the palace. Percy was breathing heavily.

"Wait. Where are you taking him?" Migo asked.

"We're taking him back to the cave where you

found him," the Stonekeeper replied sternly.

"But I didn't find him in a cave," Migo protested.

"But you said you did. Therefore, it is true." The Stonekeeper turned his back to Migo and walked toward the palace.

"But—you promised—" Migo stammered.

"To protect the village," the Stonekeeper finished for him. "Just like you did."

Crushed, Migo walked away, past his father, who had witnessed everything. Dorgle looked confused.

Then Migo looked up to Meechee's window. She glared at him and shut her blinds.

A large door of ice slowly dropped over the entrance to the palace. Migo knew that the Smallfoot could not survive in there. Saving the village was one thing, but did the Smallfoot have to die?

"Stonekeeper, wait!" Migo yelled, racing toward the entrance.

But the ice door dropped in front of him, blocking his way. The Stonekeeper looked at him through the see-through barrier. Next to him, Thorp placed Percy into a box made of ice.

"You've done your job, Migo," the Stonekeeper said. "Go home."

11

Chapter Fourteen
Where's Meechee?

Dorgle thought it would be best to let Migo have some space, so he watched as his son wandered away from the palace. But Migo didn't turn up for supper, and he didn't come home when the Great Sky Snail left the sky and everything became dark. Dorgle fell asleep, hoping Migo was all right.

A noise woke him while it was still dark. He looked out onto the launchpad and saw Migo, wearing his helmet in the Gong Ringer's chair, and staring blankly forward.

"Migo, what's wrong?" Dorgle asked. "What are you doing?"

"I was thinking about Stone Fifteen," Migo replied.

"Stone Fifteen? 'Ignorance is bliss'?" Dorgle asked.

Migo nodded. "That one is true. Ignorance *is* bliss. Or at least, it was. It was bliss not to know about the Smallfoot, and what great friends the S.E.S. would be, and how amazing Meechee is. It would be bliss not to know that they hate me and that the Smallfoot is locked in the Stonekeeper's palace and will probably never get home."

He looked at his dad. "And remember when we had a Sky Snail to wake up? And you had the most important job in the village? Before I blew it?" He sighed. "I miss being ignorant."

He tightened the strap on his helmet. "So, let's go back to the way it was. But I'll be Gong Ringer from now on. Hopefully, banging my head into that thing will make all these feelings go away."

"Oh yeah, you'll pretty much go numb," Dorgle agreed. "You won't feel a thing."

"Good. 'Cause I feel like such an idiot," Migo said.

Dorgle looked at the gong, and then at the palace. "Okay," he said. "Let's do it."

He started to crank the launch wheel. "Now, you remember the advice I gave you, right? First you gotta check the wind. Pretty easy to be blown off course."

"Wind. Check," Migo said in a lifeless voice.

"And you've gotta true your aim," Dorgle reminded him. "You'll mess up big-time if your aim isn't true."

"Aim. Check."

"And don't forget, even though you know it's gonna hurt, you gotta hit it head-on," Dorgle finished.

He turned the crank, and Migo's chair moved so that he faced the palace, not the gong. He looked back at his dad.

"You already woke the village, Son," Dorgle said. "Now make sure they stay awake." He put his hand on the release lever, and Migo smiled.

When Migo had thought that by lying about the Smallfoot he'd been doing what was best for everyone, he'd made that decision out of fear. There had to be another way—a way that didn't mean everyone had to push down their questions. A way that didn't mean the Smallfoot would have to die.

It wasn't too late.

"I love you, Dad," Migo said.

"I love you too," Dorgle replied.

Thwang! He fired Migo off the launchpad.

Migo soared across the village, past the gong, and right through Meechee's window! He slammed his head against the wall, fell back, and then jumped up. He touched his head gently.

"Yep, it does hurt," he said. "Meechee, I'm so sorry."

Blossom the mammoth stared blankly at him. Meechee was not there.

"Oh no, no, no," Migo said. Then he spotted something on the wall—something that made his cold blood turn to ice. At that moment the Stonekeeper rushed in.

"Meechee?" he asked, and then he saw Migo. "What are you doing here? Where's my daughter?"

He followed Migo's gaze to the wall of Percy's drawings of the human world. But one had been drawn by Meechee's hand. It showed a Yeti holding a human, and it had an arrow pointing down below the clouds.

"Meechee!" the Stonekeeper cried.

"Where's the Smallfoot?" Migo asked.

They rushed out of the room and into the great hall, where Thorp sat next to the block of ice that had held the Smallfoot.

"Yeah, so Meechee took the Smallfoot and convinced me I have a lot of anger issues because of something called a 'father complex,'" Thorp explained. "I don't know. I'm doing some serious processing right now, Dad."

Migo knew exactly where Meechee was headed. He raced out of the palace to the edge of the ice cliffs, where he found Gwangi, Kolka, and Fleem gazing over the edge.

"Guys! Guys! You have to help me!" Migo pleaded. "Meechee's taken the Smallfoot below the clouds!"

They ignored him.

"Look, I'm sorry," Migo said. "I didn't mean what I said. I can explain everything—after we find Meechee. She's in danger. You have to believe me!"

"Why should we believe you?" Kolka asked. "You lied. Friends don't do that."

"Or stab you in the back and call you crazy in front of the whole village," Gwangi added.

"You acted like me," Fleem told Migo. "I expected more from you."

"You're right. I lied," Migo admitted. "You know, you've always searched for the truth, no matter what anybody said. They laughed at you. They called you names."

"Wait, what names?" Fleem asked.

"But you never let fear get in the way," Migo said. "That's what I should have done."

He sighed as he looked out over the clouds. "And it's what I'm going to do now."

With a look of determination on his face, he ran toward the edge of the cliff and jumped off.

"Migo!" Gwangi and Kolka yelled.

"Wait! What names?" Fleem yelled after Migo.

Migo fell . . . and fell . . . and fell . . . and landed in the same spot where he'd landed the first time, right next to the goat. The creature leaped out of the way just in time as Migo hit the ground, kicking up an explosion of snow.

"Meechee, where are you?" he asked as he crawled out of the snowdrift.

Then he heard a cry from up above.

"Aaaaaahhhhhhhhh!"

Whomp! Kolka landed on top of him.

"Kolka!" Migo cried, shaking off more snow.

"Hi," Kolka said.

"Hi!" Migo replied, happy to see her. Then he realized something. "Wait, if you're here, then that means . . ."

"Aaaaaaaaaaaah!"

WHAM! Gwangi landed on top of both of them, creating a huge crater in the snowscape.

"Man, that was a long way down," Gwangi remarked.

They all stood up.

"Guys! You came!" Migo said.

"Of course we came," Kolka said, "for *Meechee*."

"Ah, yeah, I knew that," Migo said sheepishly.

"And a little bit for you," Kolka added. "But mostly Meechee."

"Thank you," Migo said. "Even you, Fleem. Wait, where's Fleem?"

The short Yeti was still on top of the cliff's edge, peering down.

"Okay, pros and cons," he coached himself. "Pros—Migo needs you. Cons—you're useless to him if you're dead. Cons, one. Pros, zero. Okay . . ."

"Yeah, he has serious character issues," Gwangi explained, nodding his head.

"We can't wait," Migo said. "We have to find Meechee right now before someone else does."

They crawled up and out of the crater. Kolka and

Gwangi marveled at the world below the clouds.

"Wow, it's so big," Kolka said, her eyes wide.

"How do we even know she landed here?" Gwangi asked.

His question was answered by a Meechee-shaped hole in the snow right in front of them.

"Let's follow her trail," Migo said, and the three Yetis set off to find their friend.

Chapter Fifteen
Meechee in the City

Meechee, meanwhile, had stuffed Percy into a sack and had tied him to her with a rope, the way she'd seen Migo do. She traveled down the mountain carefully, checking on Percy every few minutes to make sure he was okay.

When she reached the bottom of the mountain, she followed sounds and lights until she reached the human city. She saw a human building with steam coming out of a vent on the side. She put some cardboard boxes together to make a crude bed for the Smallfoot and laid him down on them.

Very quickly he began to breathe more easily, and the pink color returned to his cheeks.

"Okay, little guy. You can breathe easy now. See?

You're home now," Meechee said. "You can relax."

She stared at Percy for a few moments, making sure he was okay.

Thump! Thump! Thump!

The rhythmic beat of electronic music floated through the air. Curious, Meechee walked away, heading toward the sound of the music.

Percy's eyes fluttered open. "Ahhh, I can breathe," he said gratefully. A red neon sign blinking the word "Coffee" made him squint. "Where am I?"

He leaped up and saw that he was back in the human village.

"Wait. If I'm here, then where . . . ?"

He suddenly saw Meechee. She was strolling down the street, past the shops, curiously looking into windows.

"She saved my life," Percy realized.

People started to poke their heads out of their doors, astonished by the site of the furry creature strolling through their village.

"Oh no, no, no!" Percy cried.

Meechee had reached the center of town, where a pretty tree grew next to a pagoda. She felt the leaves on the tree and knelt down to look inside the pagoda.

A group of human legs came into her line of vision.

"Oh! Another Smallfoot . . . and another, and another!" she said happily. She stood up and looked around. The humans stared back at her, openmouthed.

"Hi," Meechee said.

But the humans all heard: *Groowwwwwl.*

The crowd took a step back from her—everyone except a little girl. She ran gleefully toward Meechee, away from her terrified mother. She reached up to Meechee with a tiny hand.

"Awwwww," Meechee said.

And the humans heard: *Grrrrrrr . . .*

The little girl touched Meechee's hand, bringing tears to the Yeti's eyes. She had dreamed of discovering a Smallfoot, and here she was, surrounded by them! And they were so cute!

Migo, Gwangi, and Kolka reached the village in time to see the crowd surrounding Meechee.

"Oh no!" Migo cried. "We've got to get to her before she attracts too much attention."

At his words, sirens began to sound, and swirling lights began to flash.

"Too late," Kolka said.

The crowd, who had been enchanted by Meechee, burst into excited chatter. Percy pushed through them.

"Move! Please! For the love of Yeti!" he cried.

A voice came over a loudspeaker. "Everybody, do not panic. Remain calm and run for your lives."

Police officers slammed barricades around Meechee, just as Percy made his way to the front of the crowd.

"No! Wait!" Percy yelled. "I know her!"

The officers ignored Percy. They aimed a bright spotlight at Meechee. Animal control officers opened cases containing tranquilizer guns, nets, and animal traps.

"Oh no, NO!" Percy wailed.

Thwoosh! One of the officers shot a net at Meechee. The hook that was attached to the net landed on her foot.

Meechee reacted with surprise. *Grooowwwwwwllllll!*

Her roar caused chaos, sending the crowd running in all directions. They bumped into the officers and their equipment.

"No! Come back! Please!" Meechee begged. She had no idea what kind of danger she was in.

The animal control officers reloaded their nets.

The crowd ignored the orders to run and stayed behind the barricades, eager to see what was going to happen.

Meechee spotted Percy.

"Hi. What's happening?" she asked. "I don't understand!"

The humans heard: *ROOOOOOOAAAAAAR!*

"You have to get out of here!" Percy yelled, waving his arms. But the crowd, frightened by Meechee's roar, finally began to run away, sweeping Percy along with them.

Animal control officers shot another net at Meechee. She roared and stumbled back to avoid it. A furry hand grabbed her by the arm and pulled her into an alleyway.

"Meechee, quickly, this way!" Kolka urged, and Gwangi spun Meechee around.

"Wait. You came for me?" Meechee asked.

"Of course!" Gwangi replied. "We couldn't leave you in the hands of these brutes!"

"Why'd they turn all mean like that?" Meechee asked.

Migo stepped out of the darkness. "Because they're terrible, violent creatures."

"You!" Meechee cried. "Why are you here?"

"I'm rescuing you!" Migo replied.

"Me? Rescuing me? From what?" Meechee shot back. "You said there's no such thing as a Smallfoot. Well, look around, liar!"

Gwangi and Kolka each grabbed her by an arm.

"Not the time!" Gwangi said.

"Or the place!" Kolka added.

Percy tried to make his way back to Meechee, but he nearly got trampled by the crowd. He ended up flat on his back in the middle of the street.

A man from the village leaned over him, his face gleaming with excitement. "Percy Patterson?" The man reached down to help Percy up. "It is! It's Percy Patterson!"

"Wait, you know who I am?" Percy asked.

Another man ran up and quickly took Percy's photo, and then the two ran off.

"Percy Patterson?"

He whipped around.

"Selfie?" asked a teenage girl holding up her phone.

"What?" Percy asked.

She leaned in, pursed her lips, snapped the picture, and walked away.

"What the blazes is going on?" Percy wondered.

All around him people were saying his name and pointing. He'd imagined this kind of fame before but had never experienced it.

"Percy?!"

Brenda zoomed up to him on a snowmobile. Unable to stop quickly enough, she plowed into him. *Blam!* He flew up into the air. She stopped the machine and hopped off to help him.

"Percy, you're alive! You're alive!" she cried, but at the moment he wasn't moving. "Oh my gosh, you are alive, aren't you? Please tell me that I didn't just kill you."

"Ow," he said. "Brenda?"

Past her, a video played on a screen in an internet café. Percy whispering into the camera in a cave, with Migo behind him.

"My video," he realized. "What's going on?"

"I uploaded it, like you told me to," Brenda replied. "It totally went viral."

For the first time she looked at him with admiration. "It was real, right? I mean—I have the suit."

She pointed to the suitcase, strapped to her snow-mobile.

"So, you found one," Brenda continued, grinning. "You actually found one! My phone has been ringing like crazy. Everyone wants you!"

Percy stared at the video.

"Haven't you checked your messages?" Brenda asked. "It's everything you wanted."

Percy's phone screen showed forty-two voice mails. He clicked play.

"Percy, baby, it's your agent. I want you back!"

"Percy, it's your dad. I'm no longer ashamed of you!"

"Percy Patterson, this is Mark Burton from the National Geographic Society. Call me!"

The video in the internet café played on a loop. The likes kept coming. Thousands . . . then hundreds of thousands . . . then millions!

"Percy, it's Gail at the network. I want you. And if you can actually get that Yeti live? In person? I want you bad. And I'll pay."

His wildest dreams were coming true, and it was all because of the Yetis. He was famous. Adored. Admired. Respected.

Rooooooaaaaaaaaaaaaaaaaar!

He knew that sound. Percy whipped around to see Migo far down the street, running after the Yeti who had helped him, and two others.

He took off after them.

Chapter Sixteen
On the Run

The four Yetis ran through the streets of the village. Sirens wailed in the distance. When the Yetis were sure the humans were no longer behind them, they ducked into a dark alley and stopped, panting.

"Look, I know you're mad at me, but I needed to protect you," Migo explained to Meechee in a loud whisper.

Both Gwangi and Kolka had had enough of their friends' bickering. "SHUSH!"

They continued to move through the alleys, out of sight, but the sound of the sirens was getting closer.

"You lied, and you sold us out," Meechee said to Migo.

"To protect you from *this*!" Migo insisted loudly.

"If we're gonna make it out of here, we need to remain quiet and inconspicuous," Kolka said.

Meechee frowned, but she nodded in agreement. Migo did the same. The four Yetis began to move again, but—

"Tiny Smallfoot creatures!"

They stopped and turned around. Fleem stood on top of a building, yelling at the humans below.

"Fear me! I am your god!" Fleem cried.

Panicked, the humans fled, clearing the street. Migo, Meechee, Gwangi, and Kolka ran up to him.

"Fleem, what are you doing?" Gwangi asked.

"Oh hey, guys! I jumped!" Fleem replied proudly. "Shows real growth, right?"

"I am Fleem the brave and selfless!" he cheered.

Police cars zoomed around the corner, and the five Yetis broke into a run. They turned a corner—and hit a dead end.

They turned around as the headlights of a police car shone right on them. Defeated, they held up their arms.

The police car backed up and drove away! Migo turned to see that they were standing in front of a huge billboard for the Yeti Museum. They had blended right in!

Crunch! Gwangi backed up too far and punched a hole in the billboard, then fell backward into the building behind it. Curious, the other Yetis climbed through.

It was dark inside the museum as the five Yetis slowly walked through it, studying the displays. Horrifying statues of Yetis with snarling faces stared back at them.

Fleem bumped into a statue and cried out in fear. "Ahhhhh!"

He turned and faced a mural that showed a monstrous Yeti breathing fire.

He jumped back, frightened. "Ahhhhh! Scary!"

Fleem bumped into another statue. "Ahhh! Hideous!"

Gwangi stepped out of a shadow. "It's not a statue. It's me, Fleem."

"I know," Fleem replied. "Aaaaaahhhhh!"

Meechee stared at a painting on the wall showing humans with weapons conquering the Yetis. Migo came up beside her.

"This is what your dad showed me," he explained. "This is why I lied."

"I . . . I don't understand," she said. "Why would humans want to conquer Yetis?"

She moved to a display of a 3-D model of a human village. She pressed a button, and mechanical Yetis popped up. Gnashing their teeth, they chased the humans.

"Horrible. They think *we're* monsters," Meechee realized. "But we would never do anything like this."

Then she and Migo gazed at the huge hole that Gwangi had punched in the wall. Outside stretched a path of broken cars, smashed satellite dishes, and pieces of buildings, all destroyed in their race to escape the police and the angry mob.

"Oh," they both said.

Lights flashed through the museum windows.

"They're gonna find us!" Kolka said.

Meechee still hated the idea of running from them. "Are they really all bad?"

Migo looked down at his toe, which still had the bandage Percy had placed there. "I don't know," he replied. "But we've got to get out of here."

"But how? They're everywhere," she reminded him.

Gwangi gazed up toward the roof, where the moon shone through a skylight.

The police weren't the only ones looking for the Yetis. Percy and Brenda zipped through the streets on her snowmobile, following the police vehicles and the crowd.

Brenda came to a stop, and they jumped off. "I swear they came this way," she said. "Where could they have gone."

Whoosh! Whoosh! Their eyes followed the sound. Five Yetis jumped right over their heads, from rooftop to rooftop!

"That's where!" Percy cried.

Four police cars whizzed past. They saw the Yetis too.

"Oh no. They're going to get caught!" Brenda said.

Percy jumped back onto the snowmobile. "Not if I get there first."

"No, Percy, don't!" Brenda cried.

"They're not gonna get them before I do!" he called behind him as he zipped away.

The Yetis swiftly reached the outskirts of the village and ran across a field of snow. The police cars couldn't follow. Relieved, the Yetis forged ahead into a forest of trees.

Thwap! Thwap! Thwap!

133

A strange sound filled the air, and then lights shone on them from overhead.

"What are those things?" Gwangi asked, squinting in the bright light. They looked like giant, metal birds, with a spinning blade on top.

Three helicopters surrounded the Yetis, cutting them off from the mountain.

"We're trapped!" Kolka wailed.

Then . . . *Ting! Pling! Ting!*

The Stonekeeper stood on the mountainside, hurling the stones from his robe at the helicopters!

Meechee was stunned. "Dad?"

"I told you the stones were here to protect us!" he said.

The stones bent the propeller blades, and one by one the helicopters dropped down. Their pilots emerged, unhurt, and ran away.

"Dude, yes!" Gwangi cheered, slapping the Stonekeeper's hand.

More lights approached them. Down the slope, six snowmobiles sped toward them. There were five SWAT team members, all following Percy.

Without warning, the SWAT team fired tranquilizer darts at the Yetis.

"Ow!" Gwangi cried as one hit him in the leg, knocking him down.

Kolka gasped. "Gwangi!"

"It's okay. I'm okay," he said, getting to his feet. But his one leg had gone limp. "Not okay!"

His friends supported him as they continued up the mountain. Gwangi had to painstakingly push his leg forward with each step.

Zip! Zip! Zip! Another wave of darts flew toward them, and Meechee ducked.

"Migo, are you all right?" she asked.

"Just go!" Migo yelled. He followed close behind.

Down below them, one snowmobile suddenly stopped. A Smallfoot got out and looked around. It was Percy. He smiled.

"They want a Yeti, and that's what I'm going to give them," Percy said. He dove into a huge snowbank.

The SWAT team—followed by the press—rushed to the fallen Yeti.

"Over here!" one of the reporters yelled. There was a burst of flashbulbs as one of the SWAT team members went to gently lift the Yeti's head up.

The head came off in his hands.

"This head is fake!" a reporter yelled.

Beneath the fake Yeti head, Percy's face popped up with a grin.

"Oh darn, you got me," Percy said.

"Is this some kind of joke?" a policeman yelled.

"That depends," Percy answered. "Did you think it was funny?"

Meanwhile, the Stonekeeper, Migo, Gwangi, Fleem, Kolka, and Meechee were watching this exchange from behind a tree.

"He saved us!" Meechee whispered. "He put on a fake Yeti costume so they would capture him and not us. He let us get away!"

They watched as Percy, now in the headless Yeti suit, was taken away by the SWAT team, surrounded by reporters and police. Suddenly Brenda was by his side.

Percy looked at her and shrugged. "Well, there goes my fame," he said.

"Yeah, but you have something better. Integrity," Brenda replied.

Percy gave a little nod and looked toward the hills, wondering about his friends. He hoped they were safe, and that they realized, somehow, that he had helped them.

Migo watched as Percy was led away. His heart was filled with gratitude. "Good-bye, friend," he whispered. He wondered what was going to happen when the Yetis returned home. The stones were gone, but the village was safe. And the future . . . well, the future, for the first time, was wide open.

In the old days every day had been exactly like the one before. Now every day was new, exciting, and different.

And Migo wouldn't want it any other way.

Chapter Seventeen
A New Normal

A few days passed after Percy returned to his home. Migo invited all the Yetis in the village to the Cave of Secrets, where he gave a speech. The Yetis all stared at a wall behind him filled with carved images, which he pointed to as he told his story.

"This is our history," he began. "These are our ancestors. There was a time when Yetis lived below the clouds. But then we moved up here, where we knew the Smallfoot couldn't survive."

The Yetis were silent as Migo continued. They were hanging on his every word.

"I thought the Smallfoot was my enemy, but then one saved me," Migo said. "I know I said it *wasn't* a Smallfoot, but that wasn't true. And I'm sorry

I lied to all of you." Migo snuck a quick glance in Meechee's direction. She nodded her head slightly, as if in forgiveness.

Migo went on. "The Smallfoot is real. And they live below the clouds. Clouds we make. And that's the truth. The truth is sometimes complicated, and it can be scary, but it's better than living a lie. Like, way better."

Thorp cleared his throat and spoke up. "So, we didn't fall out of the butt of the Great Sky Yak?"

"Probably not," Migo answered.

"Whose butt did we fall out of?" Thorp asked.

"You know what? We'll circle back to that question later," Migo replied.

Migo turned back to all the Yetis still staring at the wall. He went on.

"So now you know. They think we're monsters, and we think they are. And that's not going to change by hiding. We have to communicate, so it's up to us to decide what we want to do."

The Yetis all looked at one another, then back to Migo, and smiled.

Migo turned to the Stonekeeper and nodded. Together, they approached a glass-sealed lever. The

Stonekeeper handed Migo his staff and patted him on the back. Migo took a deep breath, smashed the glass, and pulled the lever.

The pistons stopped pumping.

The ice balls stopped falling.

The giant fans whirred to a stop.

And the clouds of steam disappeared.

The Yetis looked out in awe for the first time at the Himalayas.

"It's a new day," Migo said to the crowd.

The Stonekeeper smiled and nodded in agreement. "Indeed it is, Migo," he said. "Indeed it is. Let's make it a perfect one."